A Beggar
in Jerusalem

Translated from the French
by Lily Edelman and the author

SCHOCKEN BOOKS

NEW YORK

A Beggar
in
Jerusalem

A NOVEL BY

Elie Wiesel

Library of Congress Cataloging in Publication Data
Wiesel, Elie, 1928–
A beggar in Jerusalem.
Translation of: Le mendiant de Jérusalem.
Reprint. Originally published: New York:
Random House, 1970.
I. Title.
[PQ 2683.I32M413   1985]   843'.914   84-22924

ISBN 0-8052-0897-6

Designed by Andrew Roberts

Manufactured in the United States of America

9   8   7   6   5

For
Marion

A Beggar
in Jerusalem

I

T H E tale the beggar tells must be told from the beginning. But the beginning has its own tale, its own secret. That's how it is, and that's how it has always been. There is nothing man can do about it. Death itself has no power over the beginning. The beggar who tells you this knows what he is talking about.

Do you see him? There. Sitting on a tree stump, huddled in the shadows, as though in wait for someone, he scrutinizes those who come his way, intending perhaps to provoke them or unmask them. Don't ask him, he won't answer: he hates answers.

Yet who is it he is looking for in the crowd? A hunted accomplice, an adversary long forgotten? Does he himself know? Could it be Katriel, after all? Katriel: a wound more recent, a ghost more persistent than the others. Oh no, the beggar is not through with Katriel! Not yet! His denials are worthless, he is the first to say so. But he cannot be pushed. Not now, not ever. You must be patient. Everything in its own time. Dead or alive, Katriel will claim his place in this tale. After the last intruder has left the last of his victims. You'll see.

Meanwhile don't be afraid to come closer. The beggar will do you no harm, he will cast no spell over you. Do come nearer.

Do his eyes disturb you? They are not his, and he doesn't know it. His lips? They move—yes—as though repeating tales heard or lived a day before, a century before: he no longer remembers. For him, you see, time has no meaning.

Perhaps then this is the moment to warn you: if he seems strange, it is because he is possessed by a strange memory, which holds pictures and words, all kinds of pictures, all kinds of words, even those belonging to others. He remembers events but not when they happened, nor to whom. He thinks he was there when and where they occurred: he thinks all tales began with him. As for the war, he knows it's all over, but he doesn't know which war. This pains him, and he feels ashamed; now he needs help.

He is beckoning. Do you see him now? It is he.

It is I.

My name is David. Like my grandfather. Except that his pictures show him with a trim white beard, while mine is black and bushy. But was he my grandfather? Is my name David?

David: like the king remembered for his conquests. Except that he loved fighting and singing; dreaming is all I know. But like him I love the clouds, the mountains aflame at twilight or at dawn, when seized with restlessness man attempts to escape both darkness and light before becoming himself again. Dawn or dusk: the hour is the same, the call is the same; it is only man who changes. That is why man is afraid. The stranger frightens him. Not me. I am beyond his reach. Perhaps because I am his toy, not his prey. You want proof? Ask Katriel. Later. Katriel is gone. That's sufficient proof. You don't understand? Wait. You will, I promise.

First tell me: Do I look younger or older than my age?

4

Younger or older than Katriel? No, don't tell me. Don't trust appearances. I never do, though I feed on them. Look: I am watching you, I am speaking to you, yet I am sure of nothing. Not even of the moment which unites us, you and me. I cling to you to become one with you, only to rise to the surface again, alone, expelled from time, not from the tale. Thrust into the future, I feel myself overcome with pity: despite what you may think, the end is not a new beginning. As for the present, I prefer to avoid it just as it avoids me.

Here, look. A picture: a thousand shrieking horsemen, their swords drawn, unleash their hatred against me and thirst for vengeance; don't ask me why. To escape them, I feign death. Who are they? Crusaders of what faith? Cossacks in whose service? Frenzied peasants seeking what adventure, covered with whose blood? Alive I am their enemy; dead they proclaim me god. So, it is for my soul's sake, for my everlasting glory, that they repeatedly wish to destroy me and destroy my memory. But they don't succeed. My memory is stronger than they are, they should know that by now. Kill a Jew and you make him immortal; his memory, independently, survives him. And his enemies as well. The harder they strike, the more stubborn the Jewish resistance. So, naturally, they are troubled. Puzzled by its convulsions, awed by its fits of delirious fire. Poor men. They are the players, but my memory governs the rules of their game. They regard themselves as hunters, and so they are; but they are quarry as well—and that they can never comprehend. Well, that is their problem. Not mine.

Anyway, do come closer. The beggar insists. Please. Don't worry, he will take only what belongs to him. Besides, he is not really a beggar. He neither begs nor asks for anything, either from man or from God. What is given to him he gives in turn. How then does he manage to live and survive? An odd question. At night I dwell among madmen, visionaries, vagabonds of all types. My friends, my companions. I'll tell you about them. During the day they are hardly to be seen. Too busy, too shy as well. People enjoy ridiculing or pitying them. They accept it with grace. It is their way of helping others just as they help themselves. Members of a secret brotherhood, bound by strict codes of loyalty and contained pride, they make common cause. Don't try cheating them; they will outsmart you. And you won't even know it. Only the initiated can decipher the code they use to transmit information: stay away from so-or-so, he is in a bad mood this morning; get at such-and-such, he has just come into a fortune. Their occult knowledge comes from reliable sources. Their eyes and ears are everywhere, nothing escapes them. They have access to society's most obscure enclaves. But don't worry: their intelligence network is not put to ill use. Blackmail or stock market? Not interested. Glory and power? Too easily acquired. To receive is a greater challenge. Hence the poor of Jerusalem shall stay poor forever.

You'll meet them soon. Right now? It is still too early. Nightfall will bring them. Then you will find them crouching in a semicircle, on the bare ground, not far from the Wall whose shadow is the shadow of men seeking refuge in its night. With their masks on, they will reminisce about the hostilities just ended. As usual. If they are to be believed, the entire victory was their doing.

You will listen and decide for yourself. But you will not hear Katriel. You will not see him. Sorry. I shall tell you about him, but you will not meet him in person. He disappeared in battle, Katriel. The war swept him away: one wave among many. For weeks they looked for him in field hospitals and among the fallen. In vain. He was not taken prisoner, nor was he wandering around in towns deserted by man. Finally the search was abandoned, it had to be. Some day his case will be reopened. People will ask in astonishment: "Still no trace of Katriel?" I shall answer: "His trace? I am his trace."

He was my friend. We went through the war together. He did not return. So it is up to us to will his presence here, amongst us. Though the others did not know him, couldn't have known him, they will bear witness for him and in his place.

He did not resemble them? So what! Each of them has experienced more than one life and suffered more than one torment, visited many a country, obeyed certain laws and transgressed many others. Each knows the secret is eternal and eternally hidden. The roads lead nowhere, they converge not at one but at a thousand points. He who says "I" has said everything. Just as every man contains all men, this word contains all words. It is the only word God uttered at Mount Sinai. Yet one must know how to pronounce it as He does. He says "I" and it means: I who am with you, within you. We say "I" and it means: I who am opposed to you, all of you. His "I" embraces men, ours divides them. On His lips "I" means love, on ours too, but it is no longer the same love. For it is easy for us to love one another, it is even easy to love our enemies: much easier than to love ourselves.

Shlomo, an old Hasid you will soon meet, exclaimed one day in despair: "What have I gained by becoming blind, since I continue to see myself?" Poor man! He wouldn't have gained anything had he stopped seeing himself. The game is rigged; there is nothing to gain. And nothing to lose, which makes it worse. To defeat death, to defeat it by accident, against one's wish, is neither victory nor blessing. Ask me, I know.

Once, in the Orient, I talked of suicide with a sage whose clear and gentle eyes seemed forever to be gazing at a never-ending sunset. "Dying is no solution," he affirmed. "And living?" I asked. "Nor living either," he conceded. "But who tells you there is a solution?"

You will not convince me he was not right. He was too wise not to realize that one can do without solutions. Only the questions matter. We may share them or turn away from them. Either way you will in the end admit they hold no answers. Only secrets. Rumor has it that Shlomo had his eyes torn out so as to safeguard his secret. But that is a lie, I swear it is. The secret became his long afterwards. One day he will reveal it and the earth will tremble, I tell you.

It has trembled already. My friends were affected by it. That's how they became beggars and madmen who build upon ruins. I sometimes plead with them: "Enough of the war, I refuse to hear any more! Let the dead lie in peace!" They usually heed me and change the subject. Some describe their childhood passions and thus allow me to fall in love with women they have never touched or even approached; others evoke their youth and its unfathomable compulsion to redeem man and mankind. And what about Shlomo? Like me, the blind Hasid prefers to listen.

At our first meeting he shook my hand:

"I am Shlomo the Seer, and when the time comes, no matter how long it takes, that too is how I shall name the one I await. I have never met him, so I don't know whether he deserves it or wants it. But let him come and we shall see. You look at me with disbelief, I feel it. Right? You don't think he'll come? I do. He promised. That's my power over him; without me his fate would be incomplete. Whether he likes it or not, I am the keeper of his promise. Should I die before him, without first returning to him his bond and his freedom, his secret would lose its meaning. You don't keep blind men waiting and waiting with impunity. Listen: years ago I was told he had died. I knew it wasn't true. And yet I couldn't hold back my tears. Another time a jester touched my shoulder and claimed to be the one I was waiting for. Again, I didn't believe him, and yet I trembled and wept. Does that make you laugh?"

"I am not laughing."

"You lie."

"I am not laughing."

He fell silent before going on with renewed strength and sadness:

"Still he will come, you'll see. He must come. When? I don't know. Who am I to know? He knows, that's enough for me. I think he'll come after the war. You tell me the war is over? Maybe. That's for him to say. Let's put it this way: the war is over and I am still waiting for victory."

"Not for peace?"

"That's just a word. I don't know what it means, do you?"

"No, but perhaps *he* does, and that is enough for me."

Shlomo smiled and asked me to recount his own tale from the beginning. He listened attentively and commented briefly: "It's not you I am waiting for. Sorry, friend. It isn't you."

That is how he takes leave of all who approach him

for a bit of conversation. Hence the hostility he arouses among his companions for whom waiting for victory when it has already been won means sacrilege and ingratitude. For them victory cannot be questioned, since they take personal credit for it. Which explains why a casual chat about how the enemy was defeated can turn into a violent argument—but who needs explanations anyway? My friends need none to argue, and argue passionately, about anything at all.

Let me describe to you what took place here last night. Or was it last week? They overheard a tourist expressing his admiration for the military: how did they do it? The beggars tried to tell him how.

"I did it," said Ezra ben Abraham, an old man who had come from Morocco many years ago. "It's thanks to my tears that victory was possible. From the first day to the last I did nothing but weep. And it worked."

"You are wasting your breath," objected Velvel, who has one eye and a glib tongue. "You think the enemy's troops are afraid of tears? Since when is the world afraid of Jewish tears? It was my rejoicing that pushed them back. I never stopped dancing, even while eating, even while sleeping. Don't you understand? Had I stopped, had I shed a single tear, we'd have lost the war, everybody knows that."

"And my prayers?" complained Zadok, an emaciated Yemenite. "You have forgotten my prayers. Night and day. I did nothing but pray. Are you going to tell me now that my prayers weren't needed?"

"Yes, that's exactly what I am telling you," answered a madman named Moshe. "To hell with you and your prayers. Beware of anyone praying in times of war, that's what my father taught his children. What I did? I sang.

You hear? I sang. That's all I did, although I could do much more. The people in the street didn't understand: how could I sing with cannons thundering all around? But I wanted them to hear me and not the guns."

"I . . . I played with children," said Yakov the Timid, blushing as always. "In one school after another, one shelter after another, wherever I went I played war games with children. I took the part of the enemy so they could beat me, so they would not be afraid."

And then, right in the middle of the dispute, the blind man's stubborn comment was heard: "Sorry, friends, sorry. None of you is the one I am waiting for."

As always, they turned their wrath against him for a while, calmed down and went on boasting. Imaginary or real, their heroic exploits never fail to move me. Though they are liars? Even so. But they are not liars. Heroes then? Perhaps. What if their concept of courage is not the same as ours? Does that grant us the right to judge them? For my part, I gladly acknowledge their place in the haunted history of this city, a thousand times lost and a thousand times recaptured by madmen, always the same madmen.

JERUSALEM: the face visible yet hidden, the sap and the blood of all that makes us live or renounce life. The spark flashing in the darkness, the murmur rustling through shouts of happiness and joy. A name, a secret. For the exiled, a prayer. For all others, a promise. Jerusalem: seventeen times destroyed yet never erased. The symbol of survival. Jerusalem: the city which miraculously transforms man into pilgrim; no one can enter it and go away unchanged.

For me, it is also a little town somewhere in Transylvania, lost in the Carpathians, where, captivated as much by mystery as by truth, a Jewish child studies the Talmud and is dazzled by the richness, the melancholy of its universe made up of legend.

Katriel once asked me: "Do you know Jerusalem?"

"I think so."

"The Old City too?"

"Yes, Katriel. The Old City too."

"When were you there?"

"Long, long ago."

He didn't ask me when that was, and I was grateful.

Rabbi Nachman of Bratzlav, the storyteller of Hasidism, liked to say that no matter where he walked, his steps turned toward Jerusalem. As for me, I discovered it in the sacred word. Without taking a single step. I saw it then, as I see it now.

Here is the Valley of Jehoshaphat, where one day the nations will be judged. The Mount of Olives, where one day death will be vanquished. The citadel, the fortress of David, with its small turrets and golden domes where suns shatter and disappear. The Gate of Mercy, heavily bolted: let anyone other than the Messiah try to pass and the earth will shake to its foundations.

And higher than the surrounding mountains of Moab and Judea, here is Mount Moriah, which since the beginning of time has lured man in quest of faith and sacrifice. It was here that he first opened his eyes and saw the world that henceforth he would share with death; it was here that, maddened by loneliness, he began speaking to his Creator and then to himself. It was here that his two sons, our forefathers, discovered that which links innocence to murder and fervor to malediction. It was here that the first believer erected an altar on which to make an offering of both his past and his future. It was here, with the building of the Temple, that man proved himself worthy of sanctifying space as God had sanctified time.

This city of unshakable memory, I admit loving it, I even admit loving its hold over me. Distant lands no longer lure me. The seeker is weary of seeking, the explorer of self-excitement. Beneath this sky in which colors and faces clash, steps in the night reverberate to infinity; one listens, spellbound, overwhelmed. Follow them far enough and you will take by surprise a king lost in a dream, a prophet who reduces life and language to dust. Why then don't you follow them? You are afraid. The beggars are not.

Yes, I must tell you more about them. In the daytime, too busy with tourists, most professional guides ignore our very existence. At night the guards leave us alone. We are harmless, we disturb no one. Not that people haven't been intrigued. Especially in the early days. Some would watch us with suspicion, others with an uneasiness mingled with respect: why didn't we go home? Surely we had a home somewhere, did we not? To this question, a vagabond named Zalmen gave the same answer each time: "All right, all right. I'll go home. Tomorrow." He spoke on everybody's behalf. But did he say this to be rid of indiscreet bores, or did he really believe it? I don't know and neither does he.

"And you? What keeps you in the Old City?" someone asked Menashe.

"A sense of duty," he answered. "I am a matchmaker. This is where the evening star meets the morning star, and I must be present. I have to welcome them at their wedding, don't you see?"

And Yakov the Timid, fingering his bushy beard, stammered out his unsolicited answer: "This is where words and silence come to terms. I like them both. Here I'm not afraid of them."

And Shlomo, the blind Hasid, his hand shading his eyelids, whispered gently: "What is there left for me to say? I have nothing to add. I could go away. I prefer to stay. Don't ask me why. I ask you why. Let's simply say that here, more than anywhere else, waiting cries out for meaning, even if at first there was none."

People have finally become accustomed to us. Once the last tourist departs, we take possession of the place. By evening we are the masters of the square which in ancient times used to be the Temple court.

From the walls surrounding the Old City, the soldiers, rifles over their shoulders and looking faintly amused or falsely complacent, watch our secret gatherings. Sometimes we invite them to come and join us. So natural is their embarrassment that we feel like laughing. We speak to them as to children: "Come, you are safe with us, we won't steal you from your parents."

They remind me of those fierce fighters I saw arriving during the battle and immediately afterwards, proud of their strength and proud of their pride; I saw them go off, erect but humble, troubled and silent, as if they had just recaptured a dream stronger than life. To prolong the adventure, to delay the moment when everything would return to normal, some came to join our circle for a night, an hour, a single encounter, a single story. Their tales sounded even more fantastic than ours.

FROM his minaret, the muezzin calls the faithful to prayer. Guides and tourists climb into their cars and buses. In front of the Wall, the pious chant or meditate while swaying back and forth, back and forth, unaware of the hour. The stagnant heat begins to lift. The vise loosens its grip, one can breathe again. The sun fades away behind a purple veil spreading over the treetops and beyond. To break the serenity of the place and the moment, I invoke the face of Katriel: where is he? will he return? is he still alive?

There comes Anshel with his usual followers: Mohammed, Jamil, Ali. Like most children in the neighborhood they are noisy businessmen. They sell pencils, picture postcards, stamps, knives and souvenirs. Anshel is their best customer. He buys their goods without asking the price. Then he throws them back, ready to purchase them again the next day.

Is he aware that the parents, their jaws clenched, are keeping a suspicious watch over their sons? No. He doesn't care. Does he feel their presence from behind closed shutters overlooking the square? Yes. He doesn't care. Let them hate him, that is their problem. He knows but one thing: he too once experienced shame and hunger. At present, he is not the one suffering. And for that he still cannot forgive himself.

I like to tease him: "So, Anshel, how is business?"

Close-mouthed, he mumbles vaguely by way of response. He is angry but doesn't know with whom. I know: with the war. Should I tell him? He would shrug his shoulders: it's too easy to blame everything on the war. The war is what? An evil abstraction with results that are far from abstract? One might as well believe in the ancient gods: thunder, rain, hate.

"For me, the war evokes a face," Anshel tells me.

"What face?"

"That depends on the day."

"And today?"

"The face of a dying man. A dying man who became a child again."

"And it's with him that you're angry?" I say, feigning indignation.

He throws me a hostile glance: "Be quiet!"

Anshel realizes I'm making fun of him. That's my way of encouraging him to speak. He sits down. The square in front of us is now practically deserted.

"I've seen a lot of dead men," Anshel says, as if to excuse himself. "They all became children again. I saw them as children, yet I've trampled over some. War is war and is the same everywhere. I had no choice. I ran, I had to run. What else could I do? So, to make it easier for myself, after a while I stopped looking at the corpses below. After a while war had no face for me. For me, war was a beast which killed men by snatching their faces. Now the dead are taking revenge, and I'm seeing too many of those faces. They are everywhere."

He takes some color postcards out of his pocket and fingers them nervously.

"But I won the war," he shouts, as if suddenly seized by fury. "Yes, I won, I can prove it: here is my booty!"

This was his third war. With the Tank Corps from the beginning. In the desert. His first tank: destroyed the first day. The crew unscathed. His second tank: burned to the ground the third day. One casualty. The captain. Seriously wounded. Anshel grabbed him and ran to the rear. A burst of machine-gun fire. The captain fell dead. Anshel remained untouched. Since then he has not stopped telling himself over and over again: "I'm alive, I'm alive, I won the war." Simple words? Their meaning eludes him. He repeats them without conviction. Beneficiary or victim of a misunderstanding, he feels neither joy nor sadness. Just curiosity. Too many events have taken place too quickly; to think of them still makes him dizzy. Tough, he? Victor, he? A borrowed role, a borrowed life. He blushes each time a Mohammed, a Jamil pulls at his sleeve. Theirs are not borrowed roles. Victors may not all resemble one another but the vanquished do. The vanquished everywhere wear the same dark haunted look, the same pleading smile. Vanquished children are everywhere the same. In a world in ruins, selling ruins is all they have left. Ultimately it is their innocence that is vanquished. Their innocence and, without doubt, Anshel's as well. His defense? It was a war between his childhood and theirs. All the same, for the victor that he is, victory is gradually losing not its significance, not its necessity, but its taste of joy.

It is this taste of joy he seeks to recapture when he comes, late in the day, to roam about the square where victory and the road leading to it are thought to be within man's reach.

"Admit you're angry," I go on teasing him.

"Be quiet."

"You needn't be ashamed, you know. Anger would do you lots of good."

Anshel withdraws and doesn't bother to react. I wonder how Katriel would have spoken about the war, the victory. Only once had I seen him angry. You'll hear about that later. But now I wonder how to keep the promise I made him: to say what he could not say, to save him and his tale from distortion and oblivion. I wonder whether he is alive, whether he ever was.

It is growing late. The incandescent sky turns blue, then dark gray. In its flight, the sun leaves behind thick clouds streaked with red and yellow gold. Behind the ramparts, beneath the turrets, clusters of shadows move in silence as if to pave the way for the oncoming night.

In front of the Wall, the last worshippers say their evening prayers by flickering candlelight. Several of our companions have already joined us. In a gesture of fury, Anshel suddenly flings his postcards to the ground, shouting: "Look at me! I'm alive, I'm telling you! And I've won the war! You don't believe me! You want proof? Look: faces, faces, my pockets are full of faces!"

So are mine.

II

THE other postwar period, the one in Europe, was different. Survivors we were, but we were allowed no victory. Fear followed us everywhere, fear preceded us. Fear of speaking up, fear of keeping quiet. Fear of opening our eyes, fear of shutting them. Fear of loving and being rejected or loved for the wrong reasons, or for no reason at all. Marked, possessed, we were neither fully alive nor fully dead. People didn't know how to handle us. We rejected charity. Pity filled us with disgust. We were beggars, unwanted everywhere, condemned to exile and reminding strangers everywhere of what they had done to us and to themselves. No wonder then that in time they came to reproach us for their own troubled consciences.

For years I spent the better part of my days in cold police stations. Like all aliens I had to ask for all kinds of authorizations for all kinds of purposes: residence permits, study permits, travel permits. Not a week passed without new forms to fill in, new humiliations. Survival had become a mistake, a burden. No one wanted us. Under British Mandate and still engaged in its struggle for national liberation, Palestine kept its gates closed. The American government carefully guarded its parsimonious quota system. Full of compassion, some liberal countries helped us seek refuge elsewhere, anywhere, on shores as distant as possible. We were treated as intruders if not outcasts. The victors could not face us; we were living proof of their complicity. As for the neutrals, they naturally remained neutral. Unconcerned.

Rejected by both the living and the dead, I decided one day to return to my native town, without knowing exactly what I hoped to find there; I was afraid to know. Perhaps I was drawn by the child I once had been, the one I left behind as guardian of his innocence and mine. I didn't know that he had been seized by madmen, that he was their prisoner, as was my town itself.

I wandered aimlessly—as though in a dream—through my old neighborhood, the world of my childhood. I prowled around my house; in the yard near the porch a dog was howling as if to chase away returning ghosts and thieves. Compelled to look at everything, to take in everything, I walked and walked for hours, crossing and recrossing streets and squares, going from shock to shock, from pain to pain, hoping that sooner or later someone would wake me up and ask what I wanted to do, and where, and when. No one recognized me, I recognized no one. Yet there was a child waiting for me in my past and I was afraid to follow him; I knew one of us was dead. I also knew that he alone could lead me to our teachers, who, dressed in mourning, seeing but unseen, waited motionless at crossroads, silently judging the passers-by.

Somehow I learned that three survivors of the Jewish community, the only ones to have escaped deportation, were in the insane asylum.

I knew the way. Years ago, on Saturday afternoons, especially during the summer, I would go with my sisters and friends to comfort the poor abandoned wretches with fruits and candy. The place was still the same, exuding the same disturbing quiet, the same antiseptic cleanliness. Surrounded by high walls, the institution appeared impervious to time.

The doctors were amiable, cooperative. One who was particularly obliging took charge and conducted me on a tour of the various floors. The men's ward, the women's ward, the ward for special cases. My guide was proud of the qualified personnel and the modern equipment.

"Do you know the three patients in question?" he inquired, trying to be helpful.

"Possibly. If you could tell me their names . . ."

He remembered them by heart. They were old-timers. And famous.

"Sorry," I said. "Never heard of them. Perhaps if I were to see them . . ."

He pointed them out in a darkened room. Two haggard old men with discolored lips. The third, younger than they, must have been about my age. Strangers all three.

"Perhaps if I were to speak to them . . ."

Tactfully the doctor let me enter the room alone. The old men seemed glad to see me, and not the least bit surprised.

"How nice of you to come. We were waiting for you."

On seeing my dazed expression, they hastened to add: "Of course, we knew you'd come! It's Saturday today! You always come to visit us on Saturdays, don't you?"

And with palms outstretched, they claimed their due: gifts for the Sabbath.

"I'm sorry," I said, blushing. "I'm sorry, but I haven't brought you anything. I'm sorry, but today is Thursday."

I had to explain: Saturday is no longer the holiest day of the week, it's just a day like any other. Vanished and destroyed, the holiness of Shabbat. The seventh day is no longer a symbol of the Creator's interest in His creation.

"Forgive me," I said. "The Sabbath Queen has gone away and will not be back so soon. Forgive me, but it's the King's fault."

The two old men listened politely, exchanging looks. Their repeated winks puzzled me. Perplexed, I fell silent, and they broke into peals of laughter. I was still wondering why when the younger man drew me into a corner and whispered: "Poor fellows! They're crazy."

And lowering his voice even more: "They break my heart. They live by illusion. They think the world on the other side is still the one they used to know."

And then he winked too.

The old men went on laughing and laughing, convulsively moving their bodies, shrieking hysterically, louder and louder, and yet their faces remained closed, impenetrable, hostile. Their eyes looked haunted, heavy, sunk in shadows. I was overcome with pity for these strangers in whose deranged minds my town existed still. I thought the scene would never end, when, exhausted as after a wrestling match, they collapsed on the wooden floor and began to stare into the void in front of them, away from them and, finally, within them.

Earlier the doctor had given me permission to invite the younger patient for a walk in the garden. It was a beautiful day, the leaves were turning yellow. I was moved by their fragility. Fall, in our town, was always marked by indescribable serenity and nostalgia. We liked it better than spring, which we deemed too arrogant and too eager to impose its rule. Fall, in our town, departed reluctantly, all living things trying to hold it back.

"Do you hear the wind?" the young patient asked. "It is chasing fall away."

A light, barely perceptible breeze ruffled the two rivers

encircling my town. I felt its touch on my hair and eyelids. I was beginning to feel sick.

"Do you see the wind?" the patient went on. "I do. I see the wind and the wind sees me. At times I lend it my eyes, which it returns filled with sunshine and freshness. But sometimes I get back eyes not my own, and then I see things, I see things . . ."

As he spoke, I kept wondering: What was the nature of his illness, had he known my parents years ago, had news of the deportations ever reached him? I was too embarrassed to ask. I had perhaps no right to force him out of his shelter.

He sensed my difficulty and came to the rescue: "You'd probably like to know why they keep me here. It's quite simple: I'm ill. Not as ill as the others, but ill nonetheless."

He smiled at me, adopting the indulgent, condescending tone of one who knows things about you that you don't.

"I'm ill, I tell you. Mad. Completely. Yes, crazy. You don't believe me? You are wrong. You must believe me since I tell you so myself. You are in the company of a madman, it is a madman you are talking to and listening to, one who is aware of his madness, which makes it worse and more painful."

A piercing scream behind me made me shudder. I turned around swiftly. In the ward for special cases the windows were dark. Was it a scream of distress, of renunciation? Whose scream was it?

"That's Miklos," the young man told me, showing no surprise. "Miklos fears twilight as much as death, even more. He screams as soon as he senses it approaching. He is always the first to discern its first shadows."

"But . . . it's still daylight!"

"Not for Miklos, not for that poor imbecile called Miklos. Darkness is his natural element. You might say he lives beneath the dark side of the sun. Night terrifies him, but he enjoys being terrified. It makes him aware he is still alive. When he screams, it is to summon fear."

The young patient saw no need to explain further. For the next minute or so I listened intently, but the screaming had stopped abruptly and did not recur.

"They gag him in order to keep him quiet," the young man said in a matter-of-fact voice.

I thought I saw the two old men standing near one of the half-open windows to my left; at moments I heard their shrill, shattering laughter.

"A weird place," the young patient reflected aloud. "Here, one person's laughter is the same as another's scream. And I? Where do I fit into all this? I am the one who listens, the one whose heart is broken with sadness, the one who sees without looking or believing."

He was breathing heavily. We sat down on a bench under an apple tree. The shadow of the distant mountain stole across the countryside, then penetrated the clouds above. Lost in thought, the young man was nervously touching his throat. After a long pause he began describing his illness, and his voice, changing suddenly, seemed astonishingly familiar.

"Imagine the unimaginable," he said, looking me straight in the eyes. "Imagine my seeing this town without its Jews. It sounds inconceivable, I know. And yet that is how I see it, as distinctly as you see me now. Do you understand? My town, so vibrant, so deeply Jewish in its soul and destiny, the most Jewish of all the towns between the Tissa and the Danube, well, just imagine that in my fantasies I find it empty of Jews and Jewishness, absurdly impoverished and criminally twisted and defamed. Just like that, overnight, my town, stripped of everything that once added luster and radiance to its beauty and even more to its misery. Deserted, their sanctuaries pillaged, the *shtiblech*, those halls of prayer and study where the piety of the poor vied with the fervor of the wise. Vainly do I look for a spark, a trace of life. I run to the *heder* and meet neither teacher nor pupil. In the synagogue, books and objects, no longer sacred, lie moldering beneath the dust. Where are the Hasidim and their equally fanatic opponents, the Mitnagdim? Where are the talkative tailors, the haughty doctors, the rich merchants and their customers, the wedding minstrels and the brides-to-be, the frenzied beggars and the secret *tzaddikim* disguised as beggars? Where are the Masters of silences pregnant with meaning, and their disciples, where are they? I feel their presence nearby, they could not all have disappeared! They are here, I know, though invisible and strangely wrapped in absence. You won't believe me but I see everything else. The buildings, the signposts, the cobblestones, the tiniest cracks in the walls, I see them all, I see nothing else: only the people have vanished. Well do I know that these are the hallucinations of a sick and tortured mind, my own, I know it well, and so I tell myself again and again, day after day. Still, I am not so mad as to suppose that my vision reflects any reality but my own, a reality both objectively true and having its anchor in time. I know this is my problem, not my town's. For most people, imagination illuminates what darkness conceals; for me, it has become a substitute. Which proves what? That it is I who am ill. That's what it proves, I don't deny it. But sometimes I get discouraged. What can you expect? This has been going on for years. Is there a cure for me? I have given up hope completely. In the very depths of my despair, at the very limit of my madness, I do realize that in the final analysis the answer has to do with a dybbuk: I am possessed.

That's the explanation: the dybbuk is the culprit. And I am the one to suffer most from it, because, in reality, in truth, my town, with its Jews and its myths, its songs and its holidays, my town goes on existing——but without me, outside of me: on the other side."

The twilight had etched a mask of terror upon his face. Was I dealing with a madman or with a saint accursed? Should I escape or should I stay and comfort him, console him? By doing what? How could I know? Still, if he is not mad, I thought, someone must be.

"Do you understand what I myself cannot even begin to understand?" the young patient shouted, gesticulating wildly. "I'm the village fool proclaiming from the rooftops that his village has been stolen; I'm the dead accusing the living of having robbed him of his cemetery. I shout and I bellow, knowing all the while that it is simply not true, that I am a false prophet, a maker of visions. Look here, you who come from the outside, listen to me, you must know how senseless my ramblings are. At this very hour, as the sun goes down behind the town and its mysterious woods, there, in the Talmud Torah sanctuary opposite the Little Market, worshippers intone the evening services and piously evoke the miraculous powers of their respective Masters. Near the main square, on Jews' Street, porters set down their loads, turn their faces toward the wall and recite the Amida so that Mendel the Redhead may say Kaddish. In the yeshiva, where the first candles have just been lit, students embark on a difficult passage of the Talmud. In a small room, adjacent to the yeshiva, two merchants are standing respectfully before the rabbi, explaining their quarrel and deferring to him for judgment. I know the merchants, I know the rabbi. I know the students, their chanting dwells within me and brings a sob to my throat; the porters are my friends, their burdens fill me with shame just as their rare moments of respite fill me with joy. I hear them all, they are my brothers; even the sound of their breathing is familiar, I respond to their faintest moan, I sense them within reach. So, please tell me: What is the meaning of these hallucinations, of these anxieties which leave me drowning in cold sweat even while asleep?"

His eyes glinted darkly. I was choking. I felt as though I had lost my way, as though I were alone in a hostile yet strangely familiar forest, with no exit in sight. Paralyzed, I watched the sun disappear as twilight invaded the twinkling huts and the crooked paths winding among the pines. A long harrowing scream—Miklos?—was followed at once by the laughter of two men.

"I pity them," the young patient remarked and his head sank lower. "For them the dies are cast. But for me? What will happen to me? Tell me, please, tell me that everything is still possible. For me there is still hope, isn't there, please tell me?"

I shook my head, not knowing whether I meant yes or no.

Earlier the doctor had reassured me. The young man was not violent. Yet in some obscure way I felt in danger. It was time to leave, it was getting late. Perhaps too late.

"What shall I do?" exclaimed the patient, gasping. "The forest is too dense, I no longer know where to turn. The wind has covered all the paths, all the exits, with dust. The two old men think the world has not changed; that is their madness. I behave like a stranger in my own town; and that is my madness."

He sighed, breathed deeply and his voice became pleading: "You who come from afar, help me, counsel me! Pronounce the words I must hear to extricate myself from hell, the worst kind of all, one of my own making."

I did not answer.

He went on: "If truth leads to insanity and if falsehood also leads there, what is left to us? How does God justify Himself in His own eyes, let alone in ours? If the real and the imaginary both culminate in the same scream, in the same laugh, what is creation's purpose, what is its stake? What role is man called upon to play during his mysterious passage on earth?"

His speech quickened. Was there a way to stop him before it was too late, for me as well as for him? His questions took hold of me and yet went beyond me. For one fleeting moment my impulse was to reveal the truth: Yes, friend, I had been in the town, yes, I can testify that your fears are well founded, yes, so are the old men's. Your town still exists, your town no longer exists. It survives only in the twisted imagination of faceless and ageless village fools . . . This is what I wanted to tell him, but could not: even the words had been left on the other side.

"For years and years," the patient went on plaintively, "I used to accompany my doctor every time he went to town. He probably hoped to cure me by forcing me to face reality. Total failure. My illness followed me, my visions preceded me. Jews' Street, that noisy commercial center where learned merchants discussed Torah and business with the same passion, bore a new name; strangers were walking there. My pilgrimages kept leading me back to a source run dry. The life of the town, by continuing, had thrust me out. You may not believe this, but I seemed to discover strangers even in my own home, at my parents' table. I began to wonder whether I myself was not somehow the cause of the outrage; I began to view myself as the Angel of Death creating emptiness around him. I know, of course, all this is just nightmare, misunderstanding; I know I'm the victim of my eyes, my ears, my heart, my memory; I know the truth is elsewhere and different, and you—who come from afar—you know that better than I, don't you? Tell me you know, say it, I need to hear you say it, I need to believe in your words, in someone . . . There is so much loneliness around me, in me . . . Help me . . ."

While speaking to me, he began to sway and chant, just like a beggar I once knew, a wandering preacher who spoke of conquering fate and forging the future; the child I used to be was still listening, holding his breath, his heart pounding wildly. Suddenly I understood the danger, its nature and direction. Leaping to my feet with a single bound, without a gesture of farewell, a word of explanation or apology, I began running out of his sight, out of the garden, out of the asylum. I ran toward the street, the town, toward life, followed by Miklos' scream, the old men's laughter, the terror-stricken voice of the young patient. I don't know how long I ran or when I stopped to catch my breath. But already there was someone waiting for me at the end of my flight, at the end of fear, and I knew it.

E V E N I N G has come to Jerusalem, and my eyes still hold the fire of a sunset unlike any other: sudden and brutal, it wrings your heart and then relents. This evening I wish it to inflict more pain than usual. If I suffer enough, I tell myself, someone will come. Katriel perhaps. He again? Yes. Katriel. Again. Do not ask me who he is, I will not tell you. Not yet.

I remember a conversation before the war:

"What do you expect of life?" I asked Katriel.

"Life itself," he answered.

"And of love?"

"Love itself."

"I envy you," I told him. "I am more complicated than you. I want the one to surprise the other. I ask of them to surprise me as well."

"So do I, but that's a secret. Keep it to yourself."

"I will. What I like most about you is your secrets."

Below, beyond the walls, men and women are meeting, separating, loving, cheating and enriching one another: life has become normal again. I have no wish to take part. Routine work, routine talk: not for me. People line up in front of the movie house: the film doesn't interest me. They go to restaurants, concerts. Have you heard the news? Twenty years' hard labor for two terrorists caught as saboteurs. A public debate on capital punishment, on the fate of the occupied territories. A government official denies the denial he issued the day before. Abroad, too, the weeks and months drift by; events remain the same. Riots, crises, conflicts and discoveries follow one another and resemble one another. Life goes on, and finding nothing new under the sun, man attempts to change the sun.

Somewhere in this world, Rabbi Nachman of Bratzlav used to say, there is a certain city which encompasses all other cities in the world. And in that city there is a street which contains all other streets in the city. And on that street there stands a house which dominates all other houses on the street. And that house has a room which comprises all other rooms in the house. And in that room there lives a man in whom all other men recognize themselves. And that man is laughing. That's all he ever does, ever did. He roars with laughter when seen by others, but also when alone. So I think of Katriel: could he be that man? I never heard him laugh, but that proves nothing. Laughter may be learned, may be acquired. Moshe, Moshe the Drunkard, the madman,

Moshe will confirm this in his booming voice. When did he arrive? I didn't notice. But listen to him roar:

"Come on! What are you waiting for? You're not here to attend a funeral! Laugh, for heaven's sake, laugh! Let yourselves go! Don't hold back! Laugh! Louder!"

He sets the example. Some join in. Shlomo protests. So does Zadok. They are overruled by Moshe. The sentries, on guard on the ramparts, halt for a moment, shrug their shoulders, resume their duties.

"Louder," Moshe shouts. "Louder! Let our laughter drown out all the noises of the earth, all the regrets of mankind."

When drunk, he is likely to grab anyone by the throat, acquaintance or stranger, ordering him to laugh; it would be unsafe not to obey. And Moshe is drunk more often than not.

"I have known more prisons and asylums than exist in this world," he explained to me one day. "They are the palaces and the castles of the poor. Mine. That's where I left my tears. All of them. Tears of joy, of bitterness, tears of impotent rage, the tears of a child fearing death and the tears of an old man cursing his youth. There are no more tears. All I have left is laughter."

Though outwardly rough, Moshe possesses a disarming kindness. In exchange for a single word, a single smile, he would give you his only shirt, his share of happiness. Let a beggar fall sick, he'll go begging in his place. He becomes dangerous only in his fits of lucidity. Whenever he feels them coming on, he asks to be locked up.

It is said that a beautiful young woman once fell in love with him. He was going to marry her. On the eve of the ceremony they were out walking. Moshe seemed distant.

"You are far away."

"Yes," he answered. "Far away."

"Take me with you. I would like to follow you."

"You are not afraid?"

"I am, but it doesn't matter."

So he started telling her tales. She could not hold back her tears. He noticed them, and the marriage never took place. The girl is still waiting for him.

Moshe's war exploits are rumored to be both numerous and spectacular. As a volunteer in the Commandos, he took part in every operation. Never bending his tall frame. Bullets crackled all around, mowing down officers and men, yet he refused to crawl or even stoop while advancing. Brandishing his submachine gun, invincible, he would lead the assault. When a bullet finally hit him, he collapsed, laughing all the while; he was still laughing when he lost consciousness.

Discharged from the hospital, he returned to the Old City of Jerusalem and locked himself away in the ruins of that ancient synagogue where since the sixteenth century a single candle had burned in memory of Rabbi Kalonimus. In 1520 the Jews had been accused of the ritual murder of an Arab child and were about to be massacred. Restored to life by Rabbi Kalonimus, the Arab boy pointed out the real assassin and thus the community was saved. The candle commemorating this miracle burned until 1948—the year Jerusalem fell —and was rekindled, they say, by Moshe. "You see, Rabbi Kalonimus," he was supposed to have declared at the time, "it's sometimes necessary to kill in order to stay alive."

Or, according to another version, he addressed himself not to Kalonimus but to the Prophet Elijah, for whom another synagogue is named.

There is a story told about a time when few Jews lived in Jerusalem, not even enough to fill all its houses of prayer. One Yom Kippur eve, in that synagogue, only nine men gathered, and for lack of a tenth they could not form a *minyan* to begin the service. Suddenly an old man, unknown to the others, appeared and stayed until the end of the holiday, when he vanished into the night. The people realized he was the Prophet Elijah, prompted to come by the pain of those it was his duty to comfort. "Well?" Moshe was supposed to have said to him. "I am able to bring more Jews here than you. You brought only yourself, I bring thousands and tens of thousands. My weapons? Not tears, not prayers, but laughter, only laughter. Admit then that laughter too can provoke miracles." To which the prophet is said to have answered: "In our day, Moshe, laughter itself is a miracle, the most astonishing miracle of all."

Once, while loitering near the Wall, I noticed Moshe. The drunkard looked unhappy.

"What's wrong?" I asked.

"It's high time they stopped," he said angrily.

"Who? Stopped what?"

"They! The angels. Their weeping gets on my nerves!"

Though his language was colorful, he was not always coherent. I told him so. In answer, he cited a legend from the Midrash: When Titus dispatched his legions against Jerusalem, a number of angels, six to be exact, came down from heaven and took up positions on the Temple's western wall. At the hour of disaster they began to weep, and their tears pushed the flames away from the stones. Their tears continue to flow there and will be stopped only by the Messiah.

"Enough!" Moshe said. "Even angels should learn how to laugh."

"Don't worry about the angels, Moshe. Let them take care of themselves."

"Then who should I worry about? Man?"

"Yes. Man."

33

"Anyone in particular?"

"Of course, Moshe. His name is Katriel."

"Who is he?"

"I don't know, I no longer know. Sometimes I like to think of my fate as linked to his. Except that Katriel didn't know how to laugh or cry."

"Do you?"

"I'm learning, Moshe, I'm learning."

"Tell me about Katriel. If I'm to help him, I need to know more."

"He is a comrade of mine. We were in the war together."

"That's all?"

"That's all that matters."

I wish that I could speak of him more fully, but that is difficult. Katriel is my obsession, my private madness. I may even have invented him. I would need proof, but no one can provide that now the war is over.

"Well?" Moshe asked impatiently. "Do you want me to help him, yes or no?"

"Yes. He needs help and so do I. But how and where can we locate him? That's where things become difficult."

Yet he surely must have existed. I even remember being jealous of him. Everything was simple for him. He had a father to guide him, a wife to love, and he knew how to speak of them as of anything else that touched him. Yet I, who had loved more than one woman, often with despair, could speak of love only with embarrassment. To me, romantic adventures were meant to be secret. And doomed to failure. Each encounter contained its own breakup. Drunk with guilt, parched with desire, I therefore avoided casual intimacies, seeking refuge in remorse and solitude. Who was Katriel? The man I would have wished to be. One who knew the boundaries between life and death, between love and betrayal. Katriel was wise and adventurous, simple and truthful, yet managing never to hurt anyone's feeling. I envied him so much that I came to doubt his very existence.

"You don't have to speak," Moshe said, irritated. "I'm not forcing you. But in that case I'm returning to my angels, if you don't mind."

It is useless to argue with him; he is as stubborn and intolerant as a saint.

L E T me take advantage of Moshe's departure to introduce Dan, who is totally different. Tall, thin, slightly stooped, he affects the dignified bearing and melancholy aloofness of the disillusioned millionaire, the forgotten celebrity. At times he reminds me of Katriel, but then, in truth, I could say the same about most members of our group.

An odd sort of character. He fancies himself elegant, distinguished. Rather than crease his threadbare trousers, he would choose not to sit down at all. Fortunately, most of us are not oversensitive to matters of protocol. As far as we are concerned, he could participate in the discussions while standing on his head.

His hands are long and slender; his eyes, which are intelligent and indulgent, seem to express compassion for anyone he deigns to listen to, and particularly for the world at large, which does not heed him. He is considered to be a psychotic, rogue, embezzler, vagabond and liar of considerable talent. He himself insists upon the title of prince, hence his nickname: Dan the Prince.

As for the rumors about his multiple occupations, Dan views them as unworthy of either denial or confirmation.

Should you mention them to him, he will simply raise his eyebrows, affecting to be hurt by his enemies' lack of imagination. He certainly could teach them a thing—or two.

Before the outbreak of hostilities, he could be seen bombarding cabinet ministers and politicians, generals and columnists with offers of financial and military aid. Using expensive vellum paper, engraved with his full name and title, he would spell out in his own handwriting a series of projects and memoranda, each more urgent and confidential than the last. Though they went unanswered, he was not offended. On the contrary, he saw in it a good omen.

"I have excellent news," he would confide to his companions. "Another letter and still no reaction. That proves how well things are going. Otherwise I'd have already been summoned up there, wouldn't you say?"

"Naturally," we answered politely.

"You see? Since my services aren't needed, it's clear that the army and the country are ready."

"It's obvious, Dan."

"Oh yes, Dan, absolutely . . ."

"Of course, Dan. It stands to reason . . ."

Bursting with energy and the need for action, he could not sit still for a moment. Transgressing his usual principles and habits, he would engage even persons of inferior rank in conversation, haranguing them with his views on matters of strategy and high politics.

Shortly before the war he asked me whether I was worried. "No, not at all," I lied.

"Good. Don't worry. Things have never looked better. Trust me. Besides, I pointed it out clearly in this morning's report."

"Which report?"

"That's none of your business."

"Submitted to whom?"

"To whom it may concern. Six reports went out yesterday. By cable, mind you. Top secret. Top priority."

And in a confidential tone: "They're optimistic, that's all I can tell you at present. Don't press me. I am not free to elaborate."

Since it pleases him, and to reward him for his war efforts, I am inclined to acknowledge his princely rank. The more so since his stories are so ingenuous as to border on legend, one among the many that Jerusalem, since its early misfortunes, has kindled in the hearts of its children, who, condemned to wander and pray for redemption, are forever asking themselves why and for how long.

The day after the victory Dan was glowing with pride: "You see? I was right. We won."

"Where were you?"

"Here, there, everywhere."

"On which front?"

"On every front." And lowering his voice: "I had to see everything, make note of all developments. Don't you understand? For my reports. I couldn't rely on others. Those I represent had to be kept informed, obviously . . ."

Why not? I thought. All of us are messengers, though we may not know for whom or to what purpose. If man be the messenger of man, why should a madman not be the messenger of God?

It was still daylight. A rapt crowd was surging across the square. In a sudden burst of enthusiasm, Dan began to talk about his kingdom. As I listened I became a child again. Yes, I knew that once upon a time there was a Jewish kingdom hidden away behind the Mountains of Darkness. Established by the Ten Lost Tribes, it was protected by the Sambatyon, the river which flung rocks up into the sky, stoning anyone who tried to cross on weekdays. On the seventh day the waves subsided: if any stranger took advantage of the lull to sneak across to the other bank, he was arrested at once and indicted for transgressing the laws of Shabbat. That is why no one ever returned alive from that kingdom.

"True, it's all true," Dan said nostalgically. "Oh, I know. Logically, my very presence should be enough to prove the contrary. But remember that our sovereign kingdom is beyond the realm of logic. On the level of reason, it should long have disappeared, and indeed it has, in the eyes of history. So what? In order to survive, our ancestors, over there, decided to dispense with history. Since it wants no part of them, they return the compliment. The kingdom goes on existing in order to defy all laws of history and reason."

I remained serious; he liked that. Laughing quietly, he went on:

"And to think that I was a historian in my native land. Yes, a great one at that. My works are still taught in the universities, they're still discussing my theories, my concepts of time; their originality is much admired. At fifteen I published my first essay on vanished civilizations. At twenty-one I was appointed to a chair. I was treated like a national hero whose every whim had to be satisfied. One day I had the notion to seek out the vestiges of the Ten Lost Tribes. Finances, assistants, means of transportation, all were placed at my disposal. After several years I finally reached the banks of the Sambatyon, alone. I waited for Shabbat to make the crossing. I was arrested and brought before the king the very next day. A brief interrogation followed: 'Guilty or not guilty?' — 'Not guilty, Sire.' — 'Did you not violate the holiness of the seventh day in coming here?' — 'Yes, I did, Sire.'

— 'What then have you to say in your defense?' — 'Only this, Sire. I know the law and I know it states that in order to save a single human life one may break the commandment concerning the Shabbat rest. It happens that today our entire people is facing mortal danger.'

"And I began to describe to him what was happening to the Jewish communities in exile, dispersed among hostile nations. I talked and talked for days. In the beginning the king and his advisors refused to accept my testimony. Finally they recognized that when all was said and done, it was useless to cling to illusions regarding the attitude of history toward the people who long ago had attempted to humanize and thereby sanctify it. A month of mourning was decreed throughout the kingdom. An army of volunteers was raised. Unfortunately, the Sambatyon continued to bar their crossing six days out of seven. Only a few could leave, too few to rescue the condemned, too few to defend themselves; they perished in battle. As for me, the king kept me at his side, saying: 'Since we can do nothing for our brothers over there, at least help me to know them by telling me of their lives and dreams." He elevated me to the rank of prince and my domain was the distant suffering of our people.

"Years went by. The world recuperated from its wars and, liberated, my native land recovered its memory as well as its place in the family of nations. I was curious, and with the aid of modern technology I established contact with its leaders. I learned that I had not been forgotten. On the contrary: officially listed as having disappeared on a mission both secret and special, I was enjoying a posthumous reputation even more brilliant than my former one. Streets, squares and academic institutions bore my name. Result: my reemergence electrified first my native country, then foreign lands. But this was nothing compared to the excitement aroused by

39

news of the discovery of an unknown kingdom. It was impossible to watch television or read newspapers without coming upon my picture, complete with commentary and scholarly analysis dealing with my exploits. Everyone decided to cash in on the news: dear colleagues who had hated me for my achievements, intimate friends whom I had never met, former landladies and society women who described kindnesses toward me which I could not recall. My name was on everyone's lips, and strangely enough, only good things were said.

" 'You see?' our president was shouting into the telephone. 'You are the hero of the day. What am I saying? The hero of the month. Better yet, of the entire generation. The White House has invited you for a weekend, the Kremlin for a parade. The United Nations requests the honor of your addressing its General Assembly. Do you realize, my dear friend and fellow citizen? You haven't even come home and they are already fighting over you . . . By the way: when are you coming back?'

"I didn't answer immediately. I made the most of the situation and its possibilities of suspense. The president repeated his question. Then, calmly and in measured tones, I informed him of my decision not to return. At the other end of the world the president gasped for air. 'Yes,' I added. 'You did hear me. You did understand me correctly. I am not returning.' The silence on the line made me realize he had fainted.

"When he regained consciousness, his first act was to impose absolute secrecy. The highest interests of the nation demanded that nothing be leaked out to the press. Next, the president convened an emergency session of his cabinet. His ministers had never seen him in such a state. Trembling with rage, he kept on repeating the same words over and over again: 'But what's gotten into him? Why is he doing this to us, why to me?' In the general tumult, one cabinet member expressed the view that I must be a communist agent bent on humiliating the current government and its allies. Another chose to label me a reactionary right-wing trouble-maker determined to provoke the downfall of the left-wing coalition. The discussion grew increasingly bitter. Having regained his poise, the president had to intervene: 'Gentlemen, gentlemen! His motives are irrelevant! Please, reflect instead on the disastrous repercussions! Our prestige, our international standing are at stake. We must get him back at any cost. But how? That's the question, that's the only question. The rest can wait, will wait.' This good president was a realist. Innumerable possibilities were considered and discarded. Having no diplomatic relations with the kingdom, the government could neither threaten nor cajole; it couldn't even transmit requests for my extradition. They thought of sending secret agents to kidnap me, but realized they could not smuggle their way across the Sambatyon.

"Finally, in desperation, the president made one last attempt. He appealed to my patriotism and then to my common sense: 'Let me speak to you man to man. We love you, we're proud of you. Come back and we will grant your every wish.' — 'No, Mr. President,' I said. — 'Why not? What do you hope to gain?' — 'Nothing, sir.' — 'Tell us your conditions.' — 'I haven't any.' — 'I don't believe you, I don't believe in grandiose heroic gestures, in unselfish acts with no strings attached. If it's a question of blackmail, then say so: I'll accept your terms.' — 'No,' I said, 'it's not that either.' — 'Good Lord, what is it then?' — 'I told you. I simply have no desire to return, that's all. There is nothing you could offer me that would attract me. Honors, prizes and celebrations, seen from here, seem pale and worthless.'

41

"The president bit his lips and clenched his fists, trying to contain his rage. I continued: 'Since you insist, I'll tell you more. Your country, all countries, all systems of organized societies fill me with disgust. Man has become dehumanized, horror is piled on horror, evil on evil. Fraternity, solidarity: words, words that don't even make one laugh any more. Show me a single group achieving human dignity and I'll hurry back to join it; show me a single peaceful corner and I'll gladly return to settle there. But there is no such thing, and you know it. Your entire universe is crumbling with violence and hatred. Old against young, white against black, poor against rich. Yesterday's holocaust will be followed by tomorrow's, and *that* one will be total!' — 'But it's always been like that,' the president exclaimed, 'since the beginning of time . . .' — 'Of course,' I interrupted, 'it's always been like that, I know. Knowledge and pain go together. The more we know, the greater our despair. The more we advance, the more we clash with the immensity of evil. What is your answer to that? It's always been that way. That's your only answer, and it does not satisfy me. I say it's high time for someone to rebel and make his anger heard by shouting: No, I won't go along with your alibis, games and deals!' — 'Why don't you return and take that stand here? Why won't you fight from within? Others have done it and will go on doing so.' — 'It's not the same thing. In the past, you see, man could escape danger, inhumanity, by fleeing to another city, another state or continent. Today there is no place left to go, no place to hide. That's why you send explorers up into space and down into the depths of oceans: the earth is burning under your feet, you are rejected by the world you have contaminated with your poison. You go to the moon because you hate the earth and everything on it. And don't boast to me about the benefits, the ideals of scientific research. Not all your scientists put together could guarantee the serenity of a single human being, yet they could easily destroy the last man's last breath on our planet. And still you seriously think that deliberately, of my own free will, I would return to your powder keg? You're all rushing into collective suicide, and you'd like to have me there with you as an accomplice?'

"The president was fuming. I heard him curse me and crazy intellectuals like me. Then I heard him mutter: 'He is mad, absolutely, incurably mad.' — 'What a brilliant idea,' one of his ministers exclaimed.

"Astounded, the president did not immediately grasp the beauty of the solution he had accidentally stumbled on. Later he was proud of it. The hardship of my expedition and my years in the desert had caused me to lose my sanity: that was the authorized explanation released by the government spokesman. And the public fell for it. They suspected nothing. To the admiration accorded to heroes was now added the pity usually reserved for martyrs. The public relations experts, hired by the government, had done their work admirably well.

"As for me, I bore no grudge. They had made their choice, and I mine. I learned to discard it from my mind altogether. While everyone thought I was locked up and undergoing treatment, I was actually leading a carefree life, enjoying the king's favor to the fullest. From my palace I could see the Mountains of Darkness, impenetrable even to the sun. 'Look at them as much as you like,' the king would say. 'In our land you may look at anything and love anybody without fear; with us, surprises never lose their luster.' And he was right."

43

Thus transfigured, Dan would describe his kingdom, which the child within me, envious and fascinated, had tried to fathom long ago.

"But why did you leave?"

"I had to. The king himself entrusted me with a mission of unprecedented importance: to come here and decide whether his intervention was needed. Bidding me farewell, he embraced me and said: 'If our brothers are threatened again, warn me in time and we shall take all necessary measures.' He accompanied me part of the way, put his arms around my shoulders and wished me a good journey. 'But this time,' he said, 'try to bring back different tales.' I can still feel the pressure of his arm on my shoulder."

"When do you expect to go back?"

"Soon. As soon as matters here settle down."

"Would you take me with you?"

"Gladly. The journey is short though exhausting. Requiring no baggage. Once you get there, you will live and walk differently. You will have stepped back two thousand years. As though there had been no Crusades, no Inquisitions, no pogroms. As though no holocaust had ever darkened Europe. Are you tempted?"

I lied when I said I was. I know I shall not yet leave this place. Neither will he. For want of desire? Perhaps. For want of initiative, of illusions? Maybe so. Perhaps he too is waiting for someone. Like Shlomo. Like me. That is why night after night Dan comes to join me here: so that I may watch him dream, in his own disconsolate and lofty fashion, about an imaginary kingdom where princes such as he are not afraid to love the night.

III

F E A R : born of war, it survives war. We speak of it only afterwards. Everyone knows that. Visionaries are driven to ecstasy by it, madmen to the abyss. As for beggars, they take pleasure in glorifying its virtues by cursing, and by cursing they also exorcise its effects upon them.

Tonight it is Itzik, a truck driver built like a colossus, who has the best thoughts to deliver on the subject:

"Let me tell you, brothers, what fear is: a beast you've got to kill before you can kill. Otherwise you're done for. He who doesn't agree is a fool not worth listening to. Did I ever tell you what happened to me? In the Sinai, near El-Arish, the devil himself sent me a fellow twice my size, and that's saying something. Ah, even the thought of it still makes me shiver . . ."

He acts out his stories in pantomime, his body playing as much of a role as his voice. I enjoy hearing them, though I've heard them hundreds of times. Unlike those told by his companions, they grow out of the immediate present. The others, having chosen to be contemporaries of their ancestors, are unwilling to limit themselves to dates and locations. For them, chronological truth or nominal truth is only accidentally related to truth. What do they care if the events they narrate happened to other witnesses, in an epoch long since gone by? We don't care either. If Itzik sticks to his own memories, it's because he was never good at history.

"He sure was a husky fellow, that one," he continues, spitting into his hands. "A gun on his hip, like me. My platoon was far ahead, and so was his. That little bit of desert, outlined by the dunes, seemed bigger to me than the whole big desert put together. For a minute there we were, stupidly face to face: our eyes mean and full of somber curiosity, our fingers on the trigger. Believe you me, my knees were giving way. I thought: Poor Itzik, what dumb luck, the last person you'll see before beating it out of this lousy world will be your killer. Then I gave a big yell, and my gun spewed out its guts. That sure was close."

"It was your yelling that killed him," says Shlomo, the blind Hasid.

"Are you crazy or something? I yelled because I was scared stiff. I yelled to kill my own fear. To kill it so I could shoot, kill, live. If the guy standing there had thought about my fear rather than about me, he'd have done me in, not the other way round. My fear was his ally, his fifth column, as educated folks would say. There it was, pushing ahead of him, cracking my armor and inviting him in. That's why I yelled: to divert his attention. So he'd think about me, not about my fear."

"It's your yelling that killed him," Shlomo insists stubbornly. "You surprised him. He must have thought: Hey, I didn't know Death yelled like that. You fired at a corpse."

Feeling his honor attacked, Itzik gets angry: "Are you insinuating I failed in my duty? That somebody else saved me? You, maybe?"

Yakov, the eternal peacemaker, tries to calm him down: "Why get yourself upset, Itzik? You know very well that to us you're a hero. What Shlomo means is that in times of war it's often courage that kills, and sometimes it's fear."

"Well then, all right," says Itzik, regaining his good spirits. "I don't know what all this means, and still less what it's got to do with me, but I'm not hard to please: apologies, compliments, I'll accept them all, and who cares what they mean to whom."

A young officer, an Air Force lieutenant, opens his eyes wide: "You . . . you really fought in the war?"

"Come on now, sonny!" Itzik reprimands him. "A little respect, if you don't mind! I sniffed powder long before you, and a hell of a lot more than you ever will!"

Taken aback, the officer mumbles a few words of apology, then clears his throat: "I didn't mean to offend you, but . . ."

"But what?"

". . . The problem fascinates me. What attracts the lightning: fear or absence of fear? In other words, who should be distrusted more in combat: the dauntless daredevil who fears nothing, or the coward who quakes at each order? The one can cause your death by his recklessness, the other by his caution. Because there is a point where weakness and bravery add up to the same result and cancel each other out."

"And where is this precise point to be found?" I ask politely.

"I really don't know.

"Well, I know," Moshe says. "In laughter."

"In prayer," Zadok retorts.

"In insolence," says Velvel.

Crouching beside Velvel, the lieutenant rubs his forehead and whispers: "You're making fun of me."

Velvel, the group's self-appointed clown, pokes him with his elbow: "You want to bet?"

Uncomfortable, the pilot decides to play the game anyway: "Fine. You are not making fun of me. Are you satisfied?"

"You want to bet?"

Betting is a compulsion with Velvel, the one-eyed dwarf. During the bombing of Jerusalem he had helped ease tensions in overcrowded shelters by teasing terror-stricken schoolchildren: "Let's bet you'll refuse to bet with me."

"Just to be different from the rest of you, my esteemed companions, I'll admit to never having set foot on the front," Velvel declares with mock solemnity. "It's not my fault; my ears are too sensitive. They can't take the noise. But that didn't prevent me from being jittery like everyone else, even at a distance. How did I manage to keep calm? Very simple. I challenged myself: Let's bet you're afraid. Result: I won every time."

The pilot, our only visitor from the outside world, displays his good manners; he greets Velvel's little story with a short outburst of laughter. Yet, not knowing what to make of it all, he looks annoyed, irritated. He wants to get up and leave, but Itzik, by leaning on his arm, holds him back: "Come on, sonny! You're not going to insult the other speakers, are you?"

How funny Itzik can be when he puts on airs. My companions are not speechmakers. To call them speakers would be to exaggerate their faults. They are tellers of tales. What they have to transmit they do with silence as much as with words. Whimsical and understanding, they ask for the floor, get it, then pass it along. Listen to Ezra ben Abraham and tell me if he is qualified to be called a speaker. Is he discussing philosophy or political sociology? Neither. He is simply describing his stormy encounter with a terrible and powerful sultan who had taken it into his head to convert him—imagine!—to Islam.

"It was horrible, brothers, hor-rib-le, I tell you. If you only knew what he offered me! His daughter as my wife and his kingdom as a wedding gift. His daughter was too beautiful, I told him, his kingdom too grand for a poor old Jew like me. Unfortunately, I was dealing with a stubborn sultan, more interested in his words than in his subjects. A pious Jew like myself, with no roof over his head, would make a wretched Moslem, I told him, and besides, I was married already. Nothing doing. Finally, at my wits' end, I pointed out that his daughter deserved to be chosen by a gallant fighter rather than a scared old man like me. — 'You are lying!' he shouted. 'You are pretending to be weak of heart and mind so as to reject my offer! You are lying because my daughter is not good enough for you!' — 'I am not lying, I swear it, I am not lying!' — To make a long story short, he ordered me put to death in the presence of his daughter and her thousand and one admirers. So I began to weep and—believe it or not—I was saved by my tears. Convinced of my cowardice, and therefore of my sincerity, the sultan forgave me: 'Now I realize that you were not lying. You do not deserve all the honors I wished to bestow upon you.' He chased me out of his palace, out of his city, but not out of his daughter's dreams. Conclusion: it's sometimes useful to weep."

"That's nothing compared to what I'm about to tell you," Moshe cuts in. "Once upon a time a very learned Christian king invited our community to take part in a theological disputation. The poor man was bored. And whenever kings or nations get bored, it means trouble for the Jews; we've often been boredom's best remedy—also the cheapest. We

49

still are. They call that practical theology. Well, anyway. We were given a month to select our delegates and ready their presentations. A month of worry and sleepless nights. Problem number one: whom should we appoint? Problem number two: what line should they adopt? Specifically: should this mission, so delicate, so heavy with consequence, be entrusted to the community's most pious or most gifted member? Should we pray for his victory or his defeat? Some said: We're not lacking in scholars known for their devotion and their knowledge, let them do their duty; our faith is at stake and it must be defended at all cost. Others, more moderate, adopted a more realistic stance: safeguarding our honor would be a fine achievement, but what about the vengeance of the king should the Jews outwit his priests? Since the community leaders could not reach a decision, I proposed my own single candidacy. I hardly need to tell you how my words were received; they provided much-needed comic relief. One rabbi exclaimed: 'I'm willing to believe that drunkards like you can be courageous, but a display of insolence would hardly be enough to carry off dialogues with men more learned—and more sober—than you.'

"He had a point there, but I had my answer ready: 'True,' I said, 'our own sacred texts I don't know, and the Christian texts I know even less; but as an impostor I'm unbeatable.' In the end I prevailed. My arguments appealed to the community: 'If I lose, everybody will blame me and my drunkenness; if I win, which should be considered as a possibility, the king will have no choice but to treat the matter as a joke; he'll have to be charitable or become the laughingstock of the whole world.' And so, on the appointed day, I presented myself at the cathedral, which was swarming with dignitaries in golden robes, austere-looking monks, fatuous and obsequious men and women of nobility. I never felt so drunk nor so honored in my entire life. I could hardly believe that all those important personalities had abandoned their usual or unusual occupations just to see me and listen to me. I for one did not listen. Here and there I caught an overcomplicated sentence, an oversimplified accusation. I didn't understand a word. What shall I tell you, brothers? My calm made a great impression. I behaved with such self-assurance and so convincing was my composure that it upset my adversaries. And when my turn came to speak, I managed to confuse them even more. With a light heart, a bit too light perhaps, I expressed myself freely, uninhibited and unhampered by any knowledge of the subjects before us. Thus I made a lengthy statement without entering into the logic of my opponents. The less said about my own logic the better. I recited whatever came into my head, but with exuberant passion. So, the fine thinkers on the other side were convinced that I was quoting from God knows what scholarly sources. It was not surprising that they ended up getting all mixed up, their arguments growing as obscure as mine. Despite its amusing aspect, the debate was brought to a premature ending, and deservedly so. And never having laughed so heartily before, the king sent me off with a cask of wine as a farewell gift, but in exchange forbade me to appear in public ever again. Moral: no community could survive without its drunkards."

"I've really got to go," says the pilot, dripping with perspiration.

"Not before hearing Zalmen," Itzik decrees.

"One day," says Zalmen, "our regiment received a visit from Yehuda. I'll never forget his words. He was teaching us the art of overcoming fear without relying on courage: 'Why pit two human impulses against each other? Better make them allies!' "

"Ah yes, there was a fine soldier," says someone admiringly.

"Yehuda? Which Yehuda?"

"The only one we know: the leader of the Maccabees."

"I see," says the Air Force lieutenant.

"You want to bet?" Velvel suggests.

"And Bar Kochba, remember him?" Zalmen continues in a melancholy tone. "The day he raised the banner of revolt against Rome, he summoned me to his headquarters tucked away in the mountains and . . ."

"I see," the lieutenant chortles. "Bar Kochba . . . Rome . . . What next?"

"A little respect," Itzik grumbles. "Understand, sonny? Respect thine elders, especially if you don't know them. Do you have any idea who we are or might possibly be?"

"Yes," says the pilot. "Yehuda's brothers and Bar Kochba's zealots."

"Ah, the young people of today," Zalmen comments disapprovingly. "They see only what their eyes take in. Bear in mind, young man, that when we fought here, you weren't even born. The Babylonians, the Greeks, the Romans, the Crusaders, the Moslems: all those wars they teach you about at school, remember that we took part in all of them. And if you don't remember that, you're wasting your time trying to imitate us."

"The Babylonians, the Chaldeans, the Phoenicians . . . Keep going, while you're at it. The list is long . . ."

Our pilot is a sorry sight. Perspiring profusely, he appears close to losing his temper. But since showing annoyance will serve no purpose, he decides to wait for the next patrol and then call for help. He will remain calm until then.

Cast in the role of master of ceremonies, Velvel leads the game and is superbly funny. The beggars join in the merriment by clapping their hands, the madmen by mumbling unfinished, incoherent sentences. A patrol on its rounds stops to listen. The lieutenant sees his chance but passes it by. Why? He doesn't know. He too has fallen under the spell. He is learning to appreciate the virtues of contained impatience and anger. The Wall, near yet mysterious, seems to breathe with us in the shifting shadows.

This is the moment Velvel chooses to pick on me: "And you, David, you've nothing to say?"

"I prefer to listen."

Still, he insists. Shall I tell them about Katriel? Confess that he too was afraid, that I had seen fear distort his features? They would laugh at him, at me. Velvel would sneer: "What a bore you are, you and your friend Katriel! What was so heroic about him, anyway? What chains did he break, what powers did he defy?" How would I answer him? How could I make him understand that what made Katriel unique was his simplicity? Afraid or not, withdrawn or communicative, Katriel was always one and the same person.

"Let me tell you a story."

"Does it deal with fear?"

"Yes, I suppose so."

"Is it true, at least?"

"I suppose so. All our stories are true."

"All right. Begin."

I tell them a tale about the three patriarchs, founders of human civilization, whose mission, it is written, was to travel across man's world, from dawn to twilight on to the following dawn, in order to report up above on the eternal suffering of a people eternally chosen for better or for worse.

One day they appeared before the celestial throne.

God received them with a smile: "What's new?"

"We have nothing to report today, O Master of the Universe," declared Abraham.

"Nothing to reproach You for," added Isaac thoughtfully.

"Yes, it's true, You have kept Your promise," murmured Jacob, surprised at his own temerity.

An extraordinary event: Israel's destiny was in harmony with Israel's God again.

The news spread quickly. There was great rejoicing in heaven. Angels and seraphs outdid themselves, composing songs and dances and hymns of glory, filling the universe with their rapture. Taking advantage of the occasion, the damned in purgatory demanded—and obtained—commutation of their sentences, and even amnesty. Satan, a realist, squirmed in his own shadow, gnashed his teeth and plugged his ears.

"The Messiah, where is the Messiah?" God suddenly inquired. "Why isn't he here taking part in the festivities?"

Michael, responsible for Israel's welfare, went to fetch him but returned at once, out of breath: "He's disappeared! He's not in his sanctuary!"

Shouts of pain and consternation. The singers stopped singing, the sages stopped meditating. Bewildered, the three patriarchs looked at one another with apprehension. God alone remained unperturbed.

"He is incorrigible," He said, looking paternal. "Too impatient. But how can I hold that against him?"

Abruptly, His tone became harsh: "Bring him here! Use force if necessary!"

This was done.

In the presence of His court, God interrogated the fugitive: "Where were you?"

"In Jerusalem."

"Were you trying to force My hand again? To precipitate the course of history?"

Pale and grief-stricken, the Messiah bowed his head and said nothing.

"Well?" thundered the voice of the Lord. "Won't you even defend yourself?"

"Leave it to him, he'll plead extenuating circumstances again," said Satan under his breath.

"I was afraid," said the Messiah. "Afraid for Your people. And then . . . I couldn't do otherwise. All I did was follow them . . ."

"Follow whom?"

". . . I couldn't remain behind. Seeing them in their multitudes, stubborn and determined, watching them go down to earth bringing aid to their children, who are also Your children, I had to join them, be one of them. Their will was stronger than mine, stronger than Yours, and so was their love. You see, they were six million."

And because his head was bent, he could not see his forefathers smiling with pride, perhaps also with remorse: a generation earlier, before and during the holocaust, they had tried to do what he did; they had failed.

"You saw him with your own eyes?" my blind friend Shlomo wants to know.

"No, Shlomo," I answer.

For a moment there is silence. Inexplicably, Velvel does not take advantage of the pause to propose a bet.

"But I did," says Zadok. "I saw him."

All eyes are on him.

"When? Where did you see him?" Shlomo asks.

"In a dream," says Zadok. "I saw him but not with my own eyes."

"I see," says the lieutenant.

It is now Shlomo's turn to speak: "May I tell you about my meeting with Yeoshua? Do you remember him? The innocent preacher who had only one word on his lips: love. Poor man. I saw him the day he was crucified. Not far from here."

"You are mad," mumbles the lieutenant. "You are all mad."

"I remember it clearly. I went over to him and said: 'It is not you I shall be waiting for.' He seemed serene, at peace with himself and the whole creation. I tried to make him understand that this was not the first time a Jew was dying for his faith. There were other martyrs before him. But they had gone to their death crying, screaming with pain. For them, for us, no death is worthy of being invoked or sanctified. All life is sacred, irreplaceable; it is inhuman for any person to renounce it joyfully, it is blasphemous to abandon it without remorse.

" 'Are you angry with me?' he asked.

" 'No,' I answered. 'Not angry. Just sad.'

" 'Because of me?'

" 'Yes, because of you. You think you are suffering for my sake and for my brothers', yet we are the ones who will be made to suffer for you, because of you.'

"Since he refused to believe this, I began to describe what actions his followers would undertake in his name to spread his word. I painted a picture of the future which made him see the innumerable victims persecuted and crushed under the sign of his law. Thereupon he burst into tears of despair: 'No, no! This is not how it will be! You are wrong, you must be! This is not how I foresee the reign of my spirit! I want my heritage to be a gift of compassion and hope, not a punishment in blood!' His sobs broke my heart and I sought to comfort him. I begged him to retrace his steps, to return to his people. 'Too late,' he answered. 'Once the stone is thrown, it can no longer be stopped. Once the spark is lit, it must burn itself out.' I was overcome by pity and ended up weeping not only for us but for him as well."

"You should have made him laugh," Velvel says angrily.

Moshe agrees: "If only you could have made him laugh, things would have been different now."

The lieutenant mops his brow and thinks he will go mad, if he isn't mad already.

IV

A FEW weeks earlier, as I stood in Lieutenant Colonel Gad's headquarters, I told myself the game was over. The war would provide me with an opportunity to veil my face and take leave, at last, like a ghost, along with those visions and fears that vanish at dawn. Gad pretended not to understand. He was overworked, on edge, harried by his superiors, harassed by his subordinates. I had rarely seen him so preoccupied, and never so tense. He explained, between radio messages and telephone calls, that a crack battalion heading toward the front was no place for someone like me. Why not? Too dangerous.

"You are not serious, I hope."

"I have never been more serious," Gad said.

I couldn't repress a smile: I had been pursuing death for years.

"You think I'm incapable of facing danger? You think I would be afraid?"

Gad's eyes narrowed. "That's hardly the point."

"What is the point, Gad?"

"Your place is among civilians."

"But there are no civilians in this land," I said, quoting that day's government statements and newspaper editorials.

"I repeat. Go back into town. There is no room for you at the front."

"Isn't the front everywhere nowadays? Don't you listen to the radio?"

He stiffened. "I have no time to argue. We'll discuss it some other day. Not now. Not here."

I wouldn't let go. "I'm sorry to bother you, friend. I warn you though: no matter what you decide, I stay here. You won't get rid of me."

He stared at me intently, made a helpless gesture, and I knew I had won.

"Let's hope," I said, "you'll resist the enemy better than you resist your friends."

Rooted in our student years, in the turmoil of postwar Europe, our friendship had remained intact. He had come from Palestine, I from an accursed land. He used to tell me about Jerusalem, while I pictured for him the world of the Diaspora, its miseries and enchantments, its God-and-man seeking children and sages vanished in the tempest.

As adolescents in quest of excitement and fervor, we used to stroll for hours through the parks and streets, discussing gravely, with mounting passion, the purpose of man, of life: how they are to be defined, comprehended and elevated. Everything turned into discovery, primary joy or source of anguish: a novel, a poem, a painting, an unknown path in the forest on which we hoped to meet an immortal teacher, an ageless guide to self-fulfillment. Together we applied ourselves to learning what distinguishes reflection from its source, together we weighed the pros and cons of involvement, together we experienced questioning, doubt, anger.

We were at the age when the slightest event is considered of metaphysical importance. We sought absolute truth and absolute beauty; nothing else mattered. We did not visit any clubs, we belonged to no organized group. Sentimental adventures seemed childish, women a waste of time, and love a dangerous compromise, an admission of weakness, premature resignation, since by definition it binds man to a single being, in a single manner. Ambitious and naïve, we aspired to something greater, something higher. We fled the simple, the easy way out. We had not learned yet that beyond a certain limit, defiance itself can turn into a trap and become artifice. Obsessed by goals, we scorned the paths leading to them; we had not yet discovered that man's nature and task are precisely to adapt one to the other. Young and arrogant, we opposed man and God, we opted for one against the other. Not for us the daily and earthly rewards; not for us the world and its terrestrial pleasures. Infinity alone was worthy of our attention.

Then the inevitable happened. Her name was Leah. Dark hair, snub nose, mocking lips, engaging smile. Like ourselves, she was a student. A foreigner. Enough of an exhibitionist to appear mysterious, or at least, romantic. Gad and I agreed that she was conceited, egotistic, affected and evidently boring. Together we began hating her, secretly loving her, until in the end we were spying on and detesting one another. Sweet and understanding, she loved us both, though separately, granting each of us the same favors and promises, at the same time managing to become infatuated with a third, thus sending us back to our friendship.

Shortly thereafter the War of Independence broke out. Gad chose a military career; I remained a wanderer. I was not meant to wear uniforms or take roots. My head was in the clouds, and I wanted them to carry me farther and farther away, as far as possible. Jerusalem, the Galilee, the kibbutzim: life there had meaning and purpose; it was not for me. Aspiring to simple pleasures and happiness was to betray the world of yesterday to which I still belonged.

"You never were a soldier," Gad remarked, as if to recapitulate. "You know nothing about handling yourself and arms under fire. What am I supposed to do with you here?"

"You're the commander, that's your problem."

Our conversation was interrupted repeatedly by the two-way radio which linked him with his field units. Officers came into the room, not even bothering to knock. Each had a question to ask, a message to transmit. Gad had endless details to settle, plans to clear and correct, orders to issue, approve or cancel. A bystander, I observed the goings and comings without making my presence felt. Only when a captain informed Gad that one of his men had fractured his ankle during drill and would have to be hospitalized, did I intervene.

"Here, friend, is the hand of destiny. One of your combat units is now incomplete; you're missing a man."

The problem of lodging appeared resolved, and to me that was the main thing. At once I found myself in excellent spirits: "We can go to war, Gad. Don't count on me to bring you victory, but I promise not to cause defeat either."

Gad relaxed. He finally smiled: "So you think I'll take you with me? As far as you're concerned, the discussion is over?"

"Yes, sir."

"And the fact that I have no right to do so doesn't bother you at all?"

"No, sir."

I explained to him why: "Look here, there are—as in all Jewish tales—two possibilities. Either we win the war and you'll be forgiven worse violations, or we lose and it won't make the slightest difference."

Gad's expression changed and became hostile. I had said the wrong thing. Gripping the table, he leaned forward and said very slowly, in a very low voice: "There are two

61

possibilities. Either you stay and dismiss all thought of possible defeat from your mind, or, if it's death you're after, you'd better go and seek it elsewhere. Understood?"

I blushed. To believe in victory? Easily said. I no longer believed in anything. We were going to be consumed by fire once more, and once more the world would let it happen. As usual. What was true yesterday will be true tomorrow. Mankind didn't change overnight. The Jew had always been expendable, he still was. That was why I wished to be inside the crucible. I was convinced that forced to choose between two forms of death rather than between living and dying, we would do no more than reenact the collective resistance and suicide at the fortress of Masada or the desperate uprising of the Warsaw Ghetto. We who had taught the world the art and necessity of survival were to be betrayed by that world once more. And this time I for one would not submit to the event as spectator or witness.

Gad knew me too well not to read my thoughts. "Two days ago," he said, "a young volunteer from overseas arrived at my camp. He was what you would call a nice Jewish boy. Clever, sincere and burning with love for his people. I asked him a simple question: what had moved him to leave the safety of his home and come here. He answered with baffling frankness: 'The wish to die with you.' He was expecting congratulations, and received insults instead. I was beside myself with rage. I literally chased him out of the office: 'It is extremely kind of you to wish to participate in our death, except that our national funeral—if I may say so—will not take place. Not now, not ever.' Do you hear me? Don't turn away! Answer me, it's an order!"

His self-assurance troubled me. It seemed childish. The facts, friend, you're forgetting the facts. The enemy's superiority in numbers, in weapons, the indifference of certain friends, the betrayal of certain allies.

"I asked you whether you heard me," Gad said, raising his voice.

"Your faith borders on madness," I murmured.

"So what? Since when does madness frighten you?"

"Madness always frightened me. That is why I tried so often to conquer it."

"Not me. There is only one fear in me: the fear of death."

"And madness?"

"There is—there must be—a good side to it. Not to death."

I made an effort to smile: "I'm willing to concede that people go to war either to die or to escape death. But wars are not won by invoking madness."

He reflected a minute, and a glimmer reminiscent of the forgotten years emerged in his dark eyes: "Are you sure of that, really sure?"

Later, much later, in front of the Wall we had just recaptured, Gad shouted into my ear: "See? Didn't I tell you? Death can be driven away, wars can be won by invoking madness."

He fell shortly thereafter.

A MEMORY: struck down by pneumonia, I let my fever speak: "You know, Mother, I am not sad or frightened, really. So please, please don't you be either. There is no need to. I moan because it hurts, yes, it hurts a lot. Here. And here. My neck. My head. My back. Someone is playing with a red-hot iron inside my eyes. Inside my lungs. I am burning up. Wait. I am not burning. Only freezing. Cold fire all over me. But that doesn't matter. I am not afraid. It won't last, you know. The doctor said so. Trust him. And then, believe me, it's not so terrible. It's not of great importance whether I'm cured or not, really. But what I don't want is a living death, I don't want to be buried alive. That thought is worse than pain. People will think I'm dead, and I'll scream that I'm not, not yet. I'll plead with the men in black from the Hevra Kadisha not to light candles at my bedside, not to remove me from my bed, my room, not to lay me in the wooden coffin, not to recite funeral incantations, not to lower me into the empty grave. I'll scream: Don't leave me, don't abandon me, not yet, wait until I die, I am afraid to stay alone in the cemetery! But no one will hear except the Angel of Death, who hears everything because everything alive belongs to him. He'll pray and laugh, louder and louder, and I'm afraid of his laughter, and also of his prayer. Nothing else frightens me, believe me."

And seated on the edge of my bed, her face furrowed by tears, my mother seems to be aging and shrinking before my very eyes. And in a low voice, heavy with pain and premonition, she whispers once, twice, ten times: "Be quiet, son, lie still and be quiet."

Once recovered, I felt immune to those fears. They did not return until many years later. But I can still hear my mother's murmuring plea. And though sometimes eclipsed during my wanderings, her face as it paled that day has never left me, not since I chose it as an anchor for my memories. Never before have I seen it so close or so strained. At times now she seems to smile at me: "You've come to meet me, I'm glad." Other times I believe I discern a vague reproach in her attitude: "I don't like your stubborn silences, they make me sad." It's at moments like these that I realize with shame that since my illness I have told her little or nothing of myself, little or nothing of the illusions and ambitions, struggles and defeats that marked my childhood. It wasn't entirely my fault. Like most Jewish children in Eastern Europe, I had two mothers: the everyday one, absorbed by her work in the store and in the kitchen; and the one on Shabbat, transfigured, radiant and inaccessible: a princess full of beauty and grace. Neither one encouraged my confidences. Days and weeks drifted by without my telling her anything of what was happening to me. Of course, she knew everything. What did that matter? Was that any reason not to open myself to her? Can knowledge replace language? Both are part of our being; no link is whole if words are excluded. Yet I had so many things to tell my mother: my first surprise, my first nightmare, my first awakening to the misery and poverty of a world in which I was slowly, involuntarily taking root. But I still kept hearing her murmur: "Be quiet, son, be quiet."

At home she often argued with my father about politics and business. She had a tragic imagination, my mother. She saw the dark side of all events. Not my father, he was just the opposite. I was too young to participate. I would take sides in my mind but only in my mind. With one exception. On the subject of Palestine.

It was during a Shabbat meal. Contrary to her custom, Mother did not join us as we made our way through the ritual songs. She seemed worried, absent-minded. Finally, before getting up from the table, she abruptly broke her silence.

"I wonder," she said in an even voice, "I wonder if we shouldn't pack up our things, sell or abandon all valuables, and go away."

"Go away where?" Father said, taken aback.

"To Palestine."

"When?"

"The sooner the better."

She enumerated a few facts: the general situation was worsening, hatred was pouring out over the country, over the continent. Evil was present, tangible: in the newspapers, on the walls, on the faces of neighbors and passers-by.

"Besides," she added with difficulty, "I'm troubled by a premonition. A kind of uneasiness. I feel that something is being prepared for us, that our enemies won't wait much longer to sharpen their knives."

They were already sharpening them, but my father, blinded by his faith in man, refused to admit it.

"We're not living in the Dark Ages any more," he replied. "Jews are an integral part of today's society, of our civilization, just as our family has been part of this town and its history for three centuries. Why should we abandon our home, our friends, as long as nobody forces us to?"

The conflagration had already broken out, executioners were decimating Jewish communities, but my father, an enlightened spirit and an optimist to the bitter end, still continued to affirm that in the twentieth century humanity could not possibly debase itself by once more condemning Jews to suffering the pillory and death for no reason at all.

In the streets and at public meetings, speakers were inciting the citizenry to get rid of the sons of the alleged Christ-killers, who were nothing but parasites and aliens wherever they happened to be tolerated. They screamed: "Jews to Palestine!" Father turned a deaf ear. Our schoolmates picked fights with us in class, and molested us out of doors. We felt less and less safe. Whoever wanted to beat us up could do so with impunity, and sometimes with the blessing of our teachers. My father's advice: "Pay no attention. There are bad people everywhere, it would be cowardly for us to allow them to dictate our behavior." Shortly thereafter a new slogan was adopted: "Death to the Jews." Father ignored that too. On several occasions my mother tried again to convince him to pack up and leave, and once I came to her defense with arguments of a religious rather than political nature: as a Jewish child, the Holy Land with its messianic reverberations thrilled my soul and set it afire. An attitude my father found more understandable.

"If you want to go to Palestine," he said, "I don't object."

I did want to go, but not without my parents. I could not bear the thought of a separation. So we all remained. My mother stopped arguing, and seemed to cease worrying. Life went on normally. Merchants were busy making money, scholars making words, children dreaming about growing up in a more rewarding world. From time to time I would look up to find my mother staring at me as though seeing the future witness I would seek to become.

Several months later I went with her to visit a famous Hasidic rabbi whose blessing she solicited every year before the High Holidays. She preferred to write out her request in her own hand after having paid the fee to the scribe whose function and livelihood it was.

The rabbi, a bushy-haired and majestic figure, used to tease her: "So you've decided to by-pass the services of my scribe. One day, Sarah, daughter of Doved, you'll end up doing without mine as well."

"No danger," she answered. "I write as well as he does. But you, Rebbe, you read better, or differently, than I do."

Her reply pleased the holy man, who laughed heartily. Then becoming serious again, he said: "It was my father of blessed memory who taught me how to read my Hasidim's requests. He would say: 'Reading them is more difficult than studying Kabbala.' And: 'For those who need your intercession and your consolation, you represent the Kotel

Hamaravi, the Wailing Wall which, according to our sages, protects the gate of heaven.' "

The rabbi took the sheet of paper my mother held out to him; he read through its contents slowly, stopping at each sentence, each word: "So, Sarah, daughter of Doved, you want your son to grow up to be a good God-fearing Jew, is that it? But who tells you God is interested in inspiring fear rather than love?"

"One does not exclude the other, holy Rebbe. Let my son fear God and love man; that's what I wish for him. Let him love God but only through man: that would satisfy me. What I don't want, Rebbe, is that he fear God through man."

The rabbi nodded with understanding and turned to me. Stroking his graying beard, he questioned me about my studies, wanting to know where I was in the Talmud and how I felt about Rashi and other commentaries. He radiated such kindness that despite my timidity I was able to answer without getting confused, without stammering. But I was incapable of answering his last question: "Your mother wants you to grow up to be a good Jew. Tell me, what is a good Jew?"

"I don't know, Rebbe."

"Do you think I do?"

"Yes, Rebbe. I am sure you do."

"Well, let's put it this way: a good Jew is someone who, thinking of himself, says: I don't know."

I waited for some further explanation, but he must have thought he had said enough. We turned to leave. Other Hasidim were waiting in the anteroom. But before bidding us goodbye, the rabbi asked me to come closer and looked at me with strange intensity: "You're young and you'll grow up. I promise you that. You'll see things neither I nor your mother can imagine. That too I promise you. Know therefore that we shall see them through your eyes."

I was too innocent to understand that that was not a blessing.

THE BEGGARS are meditating, the madmen seem agitated. Dusk has fallen over the city. Each of us, in his own way, surmounts his obstacles. Zadok is praying. Yakov is dozing. In a whisper, someone is recounting his adventures of the day: is it the prince or Velvel? Their heads burrowed in the stones of the Wall, two old men are weeping silently, aimlessly. Annoyed, Moshe gets up and hurries over to talk to them: will he convince them to stop crying? Suddenly I hear Katriel's voice, but I know it doesn't belong to him. What made me think of Katriel again? Though younger, much younger, his voice had the same grave timbre as the rabbi's. I am the link between the two.

Near the Wall, in the semi-darkness speckled with flickering yellow flames, I see a woman who seems to be seeking her vision and her way. I see her without seeing her. I do not know whether she is young, whether she is troubled. I do not know whether she herself sees what is visible to us. Who is she? What brings her into our midst? Does she want me to speak or be silent? Still near the Wall, she extinguishes one candle, then lights another, and I wonder whether her actions carry any meaning. The night meanwhile spreads its dense peacefulness over Jerusalem, the plains and the mountains beyond. Words and sounds, out of the whirlwind, disappear in fantasy; all that remains is the sad look of a mother and the name and the tears of her son who lived through the destructions of Jerusalem elsewhere than in Jerusalem.

V

SOMEWHERE in the mountainous region of the Carpathians. Not far from the spot where long ago a young solitary dreamer named Israel Baal Shem Tov, steeped in fervor and contemplation, prepared himself to ignite a movement dedicated to the greater glory of the Eternal and to the joy of His servants. The cradle of Hasidism.

A small town, peaceful, friendly, neither arrogant nor distinctive. For centuries Christians and Jews lived there as good neighbors. The parents did business with one another, the children attended the same schools and played the same games in the same woods. Only twice a year, at Christmas and Easter, we would remain locked inside our homes, doors bolted, shutters closed. Anyone reckless enough to venture outside risked a thorough thrashing at the hands of acquaintances on their way home from church. We were patient and understanding. Two such days a year were tolerable. By morning everything returned to normal.

Today it is the Christians' turn to remain at home. They are nowhere to be seen. They sleep late on Sunday, as usual. Some, awakened by the din, watch from behind their curtains. "What a beautiful dream!" they say to one another.

Aroused early, the Jews are converging on the main square. From there they march in procession toward the forest. They leave the town without looking back; little do they know that they will never see it again. One woman asks her husband: "Where are they taking us?" He doesn't answer. A schoolboy regrets having left his books behind; his father reassures him: "They'll wait for you." One man, visibly sick, sniffs the air and remarks: "It's going to be hot." A helmeted soldier nods with a sly grimace: "Yes, very hot."

They cross the forest and halt at the edge of the valley hugging the sides of the high mountain. A sergeant selects twenty men and hands them pickaxes and shovels to dig ten pits, wide and deep.

Seated on the grass, in a group by themselves, the killers are enjoying their breakfast. It is a pleasant summer day. A warm, gentle wind whispers through the pines. Pressed tightly together, the Jews are silent. Even the children understand they must behave and not make a sound. In the last rows, the Master and his disciples form a group of their own. A silence of their own.

Suddenly the Master shakes himself. A lightning flash has just stripped the veil from his eyes. He indicates his wish to speak. As always before delivering a sermon, he lowers his head and asks God to bless the words on his lips. Then, with an abrupt movement, he pulls himself erect:

"I have been your shepherd for the past thirty years, and I shall now speak to you for the last time."

He places his right hand across his heart, as if to calm it:

"I want you to know that such is the will of God. We must accept it with our eyes and minds wide open. We are going to die, and God alone knows why, on whose account, and for what purpose; I do not know. But He demands our lives in sacrifice, which proves that He remembers us, He has not turned His face from us. And so it is with joy—pure, desperate, mad joy—that we shall say to Him: 'So be it. Thy will be done.' Perhaps He needs our joy more than our tears, our deaths more than our deeds. Do not therefore beseech His pity. Stifle the cries welling up in your hearts. Be proud instead and let your pride explode, and I promise you, I your shepherd to whom you owe obedience, I promise you that the angels in heaven will lower their heads in shame and will never again praise the Creator of man and his universe, never!"

His disciples listen without understanding. Nearby, a crazy old man laughs stupidly.

Having dug the pits, the twenty workers go back to the ranks, rejoining their parents, their wives, their fiancées. The killers lazily go on eating and chatting. The arrival of a car shatters their peace and brings them to attention before a lieutenant who inquires if everything is ready. Yes, everything is ready. Elegantly dressed, his hands gloved, the officer inspects the scene. Satisfied, he turns his aristocratic, refined countenance toward the community. Climbing on an ammunition case, he solemnly addresses his victims, who think themselves prisoners of a diabolic nightmare: "The supreme hour is at hand. For you, the war is over. Soon you will know the kind of peace your living brothers will one day begrudge you."

His face impassive, he then proposes a deal: if they would offer no resistance, cause no trouble, they could go in family units, hand in hand; otherwise he would be forced to fire on the whole crowd, and that would not be a pleasant sight.

"I'll give you five minutes to decide."

Men, women, respectful children and disillusioned old people, rich and poor, learned and ignorant, all look at their Master, whose veiled eyes, mysteriously, miraculously, fill with light:

"It is God's will, I said. But is it really what He wants?"

All of a sudden he seems a changed man. It is hard to tell whether he is blaspheming or preaching faith in the covenant. Impossible to tell whether the anger which moves him is a denial of love or the very opposite: an invocation of love. In his shining eyes, under the bushy brows, the Temple in flames is reflected:

"Abraham, Isaac and Jacob, you who according to the sacred Oral Tradition walk the paths of our people's suffering, be our witness. I no longer demand that you intercede, I only ask you to testify in our behalf. Especially you, Abraham, you especially. Know that many of us here surpass you. Some of us are going to sacrifice not one son but five. Know too that the God of Israel is today violating the Law of Israel. The Torah prohibits killing the cow and her calf on the same day; yet this law, which we have faithfully observed, does not apply to us. See that what is granted to animals is refused to the children of Israel."

As was their custom in the synagogue during his sermons, the women weep and drink in his words, which they understand only dimly. The men remain motionless, concentrating on keeping their minds blank. Some of the youths exchange whispers, wondering whether the Master is not mocking them, himself and the whole world.

"Should one of us manage to escape," the Master continues in a louder voice, "I want him to look, listen and remember. I rely on him more than on the patriarchs, because he will have the courage to go further than they. I want him to become a vessel of truth, a carrier of eternity and fire. And if he too must perish with us, like us, I appeal to heaven, and the wind and the clouds, and the ants burrowing in the ground beneath our feet: let them bear witness for us; perhaps the world deserves no other witnesses."

The Master lets his eyes wander, as if to challenge the entire universe. He sees the invisible and trembles.

Remaining outwardly passive, some young men are drawing together imperceptibly to take counsel. What can be done? Resist? How? With what? With our knives, with our nails. Then what? Escape? Where to? Anywhere. And our parents, our wives, our sick, our aged? Abandon them or follow them to the altar? Opinions are divided, the fever mounts, time is running out.

The Master is still speaking, and the lieutenant grows impatient.

"What is he saying?" he asks one of the gravediggers.

"He is telling us about the future."

"What an exquisite sense of humor! I admire that man!"

"Me, what I admire are his eyes."

"Indeed, they are extraordinary."

"All men about to die have eyes like those," says the gravedigger.

"And those who kill them?"

"They have nothing but eyes. Empty eyes."

The officer laughs nervously, wants to say something, but the Master is concluding:

"Thus I address myself to you, witnesses! Open your ears and remember. We do not want to die, we want to live and build the kingdom of the Messiah in time and prayer. Someone opposes this wish and that someone is One and His name is One. We know that His eternal secrets transcend us. But does He know the pain they cause us? Even so, brothers: we shall make Him a gift of our lives and our deaths. We wish Him to use them as He pleases, and may He be worthy of them."

He is silent now. Having said what he had to say he feels

like crying, but he holds back his tears. Standing stiffly, he faces the lieutenant, who asks whether the Jews have accepted his proposal.

"May God's will be done," says the Master on behalf of his community.

The officer shakes his head condescendingly: "You're fooling yourself, old man. It's not His will but ours."

"No!" the Master shouts with surprising determination.

"No?"

"You are but the hatchet that cuts us down; we alone shall decide to whom we offer our death."

For a moment the officer stares at him blankly, then shrugs as though ready to proceed. Still, he would like to have the last word: "You imbecile, I forgive you, for you don't know what you are saying. Haven't you discovered yet that God, that's us?"

"Never!" screams the Master. "Do you hear me? Never!"

The lieutenant has had enough. He steps back and is about to turn around, heading back to his command post, when two powerful arms reach out from the crowd and grab him. He feels a cool blade against his throat and hears a man's voice: "If any of your soldiers move, you'll be the first to go."

The lieutenant turns pale but tries not to lose his composure: "You haven't got a chance. I've set up three security cordons. Impossible to break through."

"We'll see," says the Jew, not loosening his grip, ordering his comrades to disarm the soldiers.

They hesitate, and the lieutenant is aware of their hesitation.

"All right," he says. "So you'll take our weapons. What will you do with them? What will you do next? Where will you go? Home? Perhaps you will cross the mountains, all of you, to seek refuge in another town? Which town? And for how long?"

The man holding the knife feels his strength ebbing away. He knows the lieutenant is right. Rejected and condemned, the Jews have nowhere to go. The only gates open to them are those leading to death. But at least they could drag their executioners along.

"We'll not go anywhere," he says. "We'll stay. We'll fight. Using your arms."

But lacking experience in such matters, he does not spot the soldiers, in the rear, signaling to each other. He does not notice one in particular. He no longer sees anyone. A single rifle shot puts an end to the rebellion. Five young men dash forward and are felled by a round of gunfire. Then calm settles once more over the valley.

The lieutenant straightens his tie, dusts his jacket and casts a reproachful glance at his victims: they have made him waste precious time. Well, he'll have to hurry. Two aides transmit his orders to the troops. The stage is set with great care. The executioners have known their roles for a long time, forever. They adjust their heavy machine guns on the embankments and get them ready. Some check firing angles, others the chargers. Meticulous professional work. Conscientious killers may be rare, but somehow the Jews always succeed in bringing them out.

The Master says Kaddish, and as one man the congregation repeats it after him, word for word. Nobody laments, not even the children, though their eyes are devoured by curiosity—or is it fear?

A signal from the lieutenant marks the opening of the ceremony. The president of the community leads the march. To be first at all times is an honor he deserves by virtue of his title and position. Dignified, his upright, unflinching

manner commands respect. In the synagogue he occupied
the seat nearest the sanctuary. At the edge of the grave he
holds his head high, contemptuous of the killers, refusing
to grant them any importance. A short crackling, and he
blinks. He falls without bending his knees. His two daugh-
ters are still standing. Their eyes shining with intelligence
and wit, their bodies hungry for love and offering, they
remain still, a determined smile on their lips: "Are you
pleased with us, Father?" The second separating them from
him seems eternal. But everything has an end. Even eternity.

Surrounded by his disciples, his spiritual family, the Master steps forward, as if to run to the graves. But he changes
his mind: "I haven't seen enough yet," he says with a savage
look.

The notables follow. Two or three who have never set
foot in the synagogue, wishing to stay outside of Jewish
life, defining themselves as related to humanity as a whole:
"We are Jews only by accident; we are men and that is all."
Yet, here they are: Jews again. And men. Because there
comes a time when one cannot be a man without assuming
the Jewish condition.

Things become complicated with Tevye the Tailor. It
is not his fault. He has too many children, ten to be
exact. The eldest having just celebrated his bar mitzvah. Impossible to line them up in proper order: the smaller ones
cannot stand on their own feet. The lieutenant suggests
dividing them into two groups, but Tevye protests against
this discriminatory measure, and not without reason: "I have
the same rights as the others. We want to go together." In
his desire to demonstrate that justice is no empty word, the
officer helps the tailor with an ingenious solution: the older
children will surround the younger ones—holding their
hands—and thus the entire family will be able to leave the

world quietly and politely, as is fitting. After several repeated attempts and rehearsals, things fall into place, and the officer, relieved, tells himself that Jews are, after all, not quite as bad as is commonly thought.

The hours go by slowly and peacefully, the sun is abandoning the valley, the clearing with its deep red waters is being swallowed by the forest. Time is running out. Ten graves, ten shifts. Faster, faster.

Now it is the turn of the Master and his disciples. Weary, the killers breathe easier: it's almost finished. But then they are petrified as the old man throws his head back and shouts: "The hour has come! Sing, my children! Sing as you have never sung before, sing with all your soul, and let your song be heard from one end of the world to the other, and further still, and higher, from one heaven to another, and higher still! Sing, my children, for in the end it is our song that will bear witness for us!"

A dark, fervent student intones a Hasidic song: "*It is for Thee that my soul thirsteth, toward Thee that my body riseth.*" The Master joins in, his arms stretched out like a blind man. One might be in a sanctuary, celebrating the third meal of Shabbat. New voices rise, one by one, out of the huddled group which makes its way forward in ecstasy, suspended between heaven and earth, transfixed by joy and truth, to confront the God of truth but not the God of joy. Dumbstruck, not believing their eyes, the killers, paralyzed, stare at them, unable to pull the trigger. Pale with fury, the lieutenant curses and repeats his command: "Fire! That's an order! Fire!" And so, preceded by their Master, the disciples topple into the grave. All save one, who, still standing, goes on singing. A second round of gunfire. A third. The officer takes it out on his troops: "I'll have you court-martialed! You're shooting in the air!" Seized with panic, the soldiers shoot faster and faster. It's no use. Over there, the man is still singing. Finally the killers stop shooting. They wait. Sputtering with rage, the lieutenant runs toward the grave and finds himself looking at a madman: face without mask, or perhaps mask without face; naked pain, stark suffering, eyes staring with terrifying intensity.

"Who are you?"

The disciple, unaware of his presence, is still singing. The officer slaps him with all his strength; the mad boy goes right on singing. The officer strikes him on the head, in the neck, across the chest. Seemingly insensitive to blows, the disciple does not stop singing.

The voice of the killer becomes imploring: "Aren't you ashamed to sing against the will of God? Did my men sing while carrying out God's will? Did they even shout? Did I shout?"

A shadow flickers in the mad disciple's eyes. He understands. He falls silent. Biting his already bleeding lips, clenching his jaws, he tries to stop himself from shouting, from singing.

"You must understand," he says. "I'm the last, the very last survivor."

"Why do you want that much to stay alive?"

"I don't want to stay alive."

"Then why do you refuse to die?"

"You don't understand. I want to die."

His whole being twisted, a hint of sorrow in his voice, he adds: "I cannot die, it's not my fault, you must believe me!"

And he waits.

The officer lets out a raucous scream and tries to strangle the disciple; he fails. He draws his revolver and shoots. The survivor does not flinch. The killer has no more bullets.

Shaking from head to toe, breathless, he looks at the disciple and falls to his knees and speaks to him the way one speaks to a conqueror, a victor shrouded in mystery:

"You're humiliating me, you're taking your revenge. One day you'll regret it. You'll speak, but your words will fall on deaf ears. Some will laugh at you, others will try to redeem themselves through you. You'll try to reveal what should remain hidden, you'll try to incite people to learn from the past and rebel, but they will refuse to believe you. They will not listen to you. In the end you'll curse me for having spared you. You'll curse me because you'll possess the truth, you already do; but it's the truth of a madman."

And so, in order not to listen any more, the disciple thinks of his father, his mother, his friends, and hates himself for having deserted them. He throws his body across the corpses filling the grave and he begs them not to reject him.

Inside the grave, and above it, night has fallen.

VI

A SHADOW breaks away from the Wall, where some old men are still lamenting. Somber and sullen, he comes closer, moving with deliberate steps. His head seems able to hide behind stars. Invited to sit down, he answers he is in a hurry. He is expected elsewhere. He will address us standing. As usual. At the same hour, every evening, he appears in the role of preacher and messenger:

"Happy is he who unites his words and his silence with the words and silences of the Shekhinah, the divine presence which prowls about this place. Soon, brothers, you will feel its breath, let me be the one to announce this to you."

Shlomo opens his sightless eyes wide. Velvel stifles a sneer. Zadok smiles gently in anticipation of his own beatitude.

"Do what you can to be quiet when midnight comes," says the messenger. "It's of extreme importance. At midnight you will hear the Shekhinah. The future fills it with joy, the past with suffering, and I don't know whether tonight we will be touched by its felicity or bruised by its bitterness. By listening we shall know—we shall know the condition of man."

Below, beyond the palm groves, the city has veiled her lights and withdrawn into herself. Restaurants, clubs and movie houses are closing, people are on their way home. Lovers speak to each other of love, couples accuse each other of betrayal. In appearance, a city like any other. A police car patrols its narrow streets, its suburbs. The guards on the walls scan the entire area. Nothing to report.

"Everywhere else man expresses himself in the name of God," the preacher continues in his threatening voice. "But not here. At midnight, brothers, you will hear God speak in the name of man."

The messenger has spoken. He returns to the Wall, arms raised high. And I go back to my native town. I was ten and had gone to listen to a wandering preacher—a *maggid*—who had just returned from the Holy Land. Or so we thought. Pitiless, uncompromising, he preached without sparing anyone. He attacked the complacency of the rich and the arrogance of the young. Nothing pleased him. He asked: "How dare you pray for the coming of the Messiah when you are not ready to receive him?" But when he started his peroration, his face lit up as he evoked Safed and its Kabbalists, Jerusalem and its beggars, the pilgrims of Meron, where, on the tomb of Simeon bar Yohai, the splendors of the Zohar seem more accessible. Spellbound, listening with my whole being, I drank in his words, and watched him with such intensity that my eyes began to ache: I was in the land of legend.

He departed the next day, but reappeared a week later, escorted by two policemen with enormous mustaches: they had arrested him on the road, in the open countryside. His crime? No identification papers. The community had him released on bail. When my father expressed astonishment at his carelessness, he replied: "I know who I am and where I come from; I told the police, but they didn't believe me. They have greater faith in one little scrap of paper than in a human being. Well, I refuse to be like them."

Forbidden to leave town pending his trial, he took his

Shabbat meals with us and helped me with my studies. That was my mother's idea. She had offered him a deal: "You have no money, I'll give you some, and in exchange you'll take care of my son."

"I'm neither teacher nor educator."

"What are you, then?"

"A storyteller."

"Very well: then tell him stories."

All his stories dealt with life in the Holy Land.

"I envy you so," I said to him one day.

"Why?"

"Because you've been there."

He frowned, took several steps and returned to stand directly in front of me: "Know that I've never set foot in the Holy Land. Know also that I have never left it."

"I don't understand," I confessed, at a loss.

"Too bad, I'm not asking you to understand, but to listen."

Some of his colorful tales I recognized because I had studied them in the Talmud, in the Midrash: the martyrdom of Rabbi Akiba, the misadventures of Elisha ben Abuya, the escape of Yokhanan ben Zakkai. Other tales, which I never heard before, left their imprint on my imagination. I had one desire: to make them mine, all of them.

Saturday afternoons, our meal over, we would go into the garden and I would find myself wandering the streets of Jerusalem again. There we would stay until the evening sun set the red brick roofs ablaze, casting a deep glow over the apple trees and pines. Once he asked me what I wanted to do when I grew up. I had no idea. Leaning against a tree, he gazed at me sadly, then, as though discarding some misgivings, he said: "One day your turn will come to tell tales. Remember that according to Scriptures we are supposed to be a nation of priests. What does that mean? Remember:

once upon a time the High Priest prepared and purified himself all year long to pronounce one single word—God's name—just once, in just one place: in the inner sanctum of the Temple, on the Day of Atonement. He who wishes to follow in his footsteps must learn to say the right word at the right time and in the right place."

Another day, another question:

"It is written that Jerusalem conceals the gate of heaven. Do you believe that?"

"Yes," I said. "Everything that is written and transmitted must be true."

"It is also written that prayer there rises up to the celestial throne. Do you believe that too?"

"Of course I do."

"Then how do you explain that of so many prayers, repeated by so many holy and just men through so many centuries, not a single one has ever been granted?"

Perplexed and ashamed of my ignorance, all I could do was remain silent.

"You don't know what to answer," he said, looking amused. "Neither do I. Am I shocking you? Who tells you one has to pray in order to obtain favors? Perhaps one must pray in order to open a door and remain on the threshold. Don't you think so?"

"I am suspicious of gratuitous acts."

"No prayer is gratuitous. Each contains its own reward. You enrich yourself while praying. Not afterwards."

And a story: "One day," Rabbi Yokhanan ben Zakkai relates, "I was walking along the road and saw a man gathering wood. I greeted him but he didn't respond. Later he came over to me and said: 'I don't belong to the world of the living.' And he left."

Explanation: after his escape from a besieged and

wounded Jerusalem, Rabbi Yokhanan saw the dead everywhere, and everywhere the dead rejected him.

"Who are you?" the preacher asked me. "Rabbi Yokhanan
or the man he met?"

"I don't know."

"Neither. You are the road on which they met."

I had the audacity to return his question: "And you,
Master, who are you?"

He answered without hesitation: "I am the Temple, destroyed."

Noting my stupefaction, he hastened to add: "So are you.
Each of us can and must want to be that destroyed Temple.
The capital of the world remains in the world, but its
Temple covers the surface of the whole world. Each broken
heart can and must reflect its ruins. That is why we are
commanded to respect the suffering of others: one never
knows what it conceals."

At the time of our last conversation, between Pesach and
Shavuot, he sat me down before him, in the garden, while
he himself stood stroking the grayish bark of a tree in
bloom. More absent-minded and gloomier than usual, he
seemed harried, anxious to speak to me: "Here is the first
question which is put to the soul, in heaven, when it faces
the celestial tribunal: 'Have you lived in expectation of the
Messiah?' As for me, I shall answer: 'I was not content
merely to wait for him, I went looking for him everywhere,
even within myself.' In case they do not believe me, you
will testify on my behalf. That is all I ask of you. Will you
do it?"

"Yes," I said with tears in my voice. "Of course I will."

His burning eyes looked deeply into mine and he appeared
relieved, almost joyful.

"Thank you," he cried out effusively. "I am counting on

you. In return, here is my wish for you: whatever road you take, may it lead you to Jerusalem. One day you'll arrive there, that I promise you. And on that day, do you hear, I'll be there too. And I'll run through the streets and markets, I'll rouse the passers-by and cure them of their indifference, that much I promise myself. Because I cannot believe, do you hear, I cannot believe that God in His mercy and wisdom implanted this vision, this hope in me, only to take it away, only to make fun of the old man I shall never become."

He did not run through the streets, he did not fill the world with his fervor. He broke through another gate to the same heaven, and in looking back, he could see the Temple burning below, burning six million of its priests, he could see them climbing an immense blazing ladder: Jacob was having a bad dream.

I shall nevertheless testify on behalf of the *maggid* and this will be my testimony: "Your wish has been granted, but not your promise. They have cheated you and perhaps me as well. For here I am in that Jerusalem you were carrying within yourself; I look at the Wall but do not see you. Still, here is someone tapping my shoulder, telling me: 'It is midnight.' "

INSTINCTIVELY, in one shared reflex, bodies become tense, voices die down. In front of the Wall, worshippers interrupt their lamentations, and bowing deeply, wait in silence. Hearts cease beating, thoughts stop wandering. We are submitting to a senseless, childish ritual without knowing why. We pretend to be waiting for a miracle, knowing all the while that it will not occur: even here the invisible remains unseen. Tonight again, the silence will be shattered by loud derisive laughter coming from the one-eyed dwarf, followed by Zadok's prolonged sigh. Then that other one, the messenger, will return, all excited:

"Well, did you hear?" he will say.

"No. Did you?"

Disappointed, he will avoid our question and say: "I pity you. The Shekhinah speaks for man and man does not hear. The Shekhinah appears before man and he does not know it."

This evening I'm almost convinced. Challenged by the beggars, the flustered Air Force lieutenant has kept us in suspense with his own war tales. Looking down while flying over Mount Sinai, he thought he could make out, in the blackish rock formation, an enormous human shape, arms upheld, supporting the sky. On his return, the figure was gone. This was how the pilot had imagined Moses. He meant to continue his story, but we interrupted him: midnight was approaching. Moments later we succumbed to a hallucination all our own. Emerging from the thick darkness near the Wall, a feminine silhouette appeared, moving with dreamlike grace. I thought I was imagining it. "She'll vanish and I'll be ashamed to even mention it to my companions." Only, they were dreaming the same dream. Together we admired her, our mouths open in wonder, not daring to move or breathe lest we frighten the apparition away. The silence was swelling, it was crushing, gaining in strength and pervading the foliage, the gun emplacements, the mountains. Had the preacher spoken the truth? Once more I am becoming part of his legends: it is here that the divine presence links heaven to man's suffering, here that it penetrates their consciousness, here that it confers on the night its secret and the weight of its nostalgia. She has noticed us and comes toward us. I have to concentrate to control my nerves and muscles so as not to shout, or leap up and take flight. My heart is pounding, it is rebelling and wants to burst before the woman comes too close. My fear is so dark, so tumultuous, that it overpowers me and we become one. The blood hammers in my temples and blinds me. I should act, react, do something with my hands, my thoughts, my eyes; I am too dazed to make the slightest move. I am floating in the air, I am thrust outside time, outside thought, outside desire, outside myself. I no longer know where I am, who I am.

The pilot brings me back to reality. He is at the end of his wits. This woman before us is too much for him. He wants to know who she is. Right now, not later. He insists. He must know. I cling to his curiosity, I make him repeat his question. I hear myself stammering: "Whom do you mean? I don't see anybody."

"But the woman!"

"What woman? I don't see any woman."

"But look!"

"I'm looking, I'm looking, that's all I'm doing, I don't see anybody."

He seizes me by the shoulders, convinced more than ever that I am mad and determined to drive him mad too. "Look, over there, there!" he shouts. "Yes, over there, there! Don't you see? Are you blind? Like your blind friend?"

His indignation changes to hysteria. He points his finger in the direction of the Wall, which seems to be moving toward us along with the woman. There she is, frail and tense, in front of us, in front of me. Her hands on her hips, she tilts her head slightly toward the right. Now I can distinguish her strong features, her parted lips. Suddenly, in a flash, I recognize her. She is the one who has been following me, spying on me for the past several days. I have spotted

her coming and going, crossing and recrossing the main
square, watching, always on the lookout, judging me and
whoever comes near me. Yesterday or the day before, she
had glanced at me; I had smiled back like an accomplice. I
must have shocked or frightened her because she disappeared immediately. Now, as I observe her more closely,
despite the semi-darkness, despite my own agitation, I know
that this encounter is not an accident. And I guess who she
is: Katriel's wife, Katriel's widow. He had talked to me
about her and often at great length. There could be no
doubt. It is she. With one leap, I am on my feet. So, this is
she. Katriel had not lied. He did have a wife he loved and
who loved him. I was right to have been jealous of their
love. They had had a child and lost it: I was right to have
envied them his memory. Everything Katriel had told me
comes back to me now. About himself, his wife, their struggle against unrelenting misfortune and the implacable laws
of solitude, especially solitude endured together. So, here
she is. Alone. I had imagined her as being less beautiful,
softer. She stands before me now, her hair in disarray, out
of breath, and looking at me as from a great distance, from
the past and beyond. I wonder why she looks at me that
way and also whom she sees. I am about to ask, but she
speaks first:

"David," she whispers.

"Yes, I am David. Who told you my name? Katriel?
When did you see him last?"

"David, David . . . Is this a game? A test? I don't understand, I would like to understand."

Her voice, broken and humble, reminds me of my mother's
voice. That night, before our separation, she had my name
on her lips like a wound. She too had wanted to understand,
but there was nothing left to understand. That night names

and beings were torn apart from each other. Only much later did I perceive the secret of creation: only the unnameable is immortal.

"Please sit down," I say to the woman, trying to look composed.

We make room for her. She does not move. In her eyes a question burns—a question as primitive as it is cruel and essential—and I know that none of us present has the answer. I am hoping she will refrain from asking. Perhaps another time. Not here. Perhaps she will forgive, forget.

"Come, please, sit down."

I take her gently by the shoulders and force her to sit down. At first she resists, then her body yields.

"Trust us," I say. "You are among friends."

Catching her breath, she begins to study the masks and specters surrounding us. I make the introductions. Her eyes linger on each face, endowing each with a veil of shadow mingled with tenderness. Dan takes her hand and kisses it with elegant flamboyance: he is not a prince for nothing. Velvel bows deeply, respectfully, and in doing so, accentuates his grotesqueness. Moshe, more drunk than mad, decides this is the proper time to invite her for a dance. Shlomo covers his mouth and murmurs: "I see nothing. I'm lucky." And Zadok echoes him: "This is blasphemy, woe unto us, this is blasphemy." I now fear the scene will degenerate into folly. In the throes of trance, these madmen and visionaries have mistaken Malka for a divine apparition, the woman of their dreams, their love unique and lost. In her presence, all interdictions are lifted, all desires become sacred. On the edge of ecstasy, they wait only for a sign to carry her off, each one to his own secret kingdom. She allows them to dream, she may even be encouraging them. If, out of a desire for vengeance, she were to incite them further, they

would stop at nothing. Fortunately, I am here and on guard.
I warn them that if they do not remain calm, Malka will
go away.

"Malka!" Velvel exclaims joyfully. "Her name is Malka!
The queen! The queen of beggars, the mistress of kings!"

"The queen of madmen," Moshe corrects him. "The queen
who drives men mad."

"Malka! Mal-ka! Be our queen!" Itzik shouts, clapping his
hands.

"Long live the queen!"

"Long live the queen!"

Totally bewildered, the lieutenant beside me doesn't know
which way to turn, what to do, what to say. His last tie with
reality is gone. Without a word, he squeezes my arm until
it aches.

"Ask them to be quiet," I order Malka. "They'll listen
to you."

I must look desperate, because she complies. Is it an illusion? I seem to detect a touch of irony in her voice. No
matter. The others do not notice. One word from her and
order has been reestablished. I thank her and proceed: "You
came to inquire about Katriel, didn't you?"

Thereupon the uproar starts all over again:

"Katriel? Who is he?"

"What does he do?"

"Why isn't he here with us?"

I pretend to ignore the shouters. Their use of the present
tense makes me feel uncomfortable. Had they used the past
tense, I would have remained silent too. What is there to say
about a friend when one knows nothing about him, not even
whether he is dead or alive? Missing in action: that's how
he is listed on his army record. He may still return. No one
will convince me of the contrary.

"Katriel?" Malka says. "Who is he? I would like to hear about him."

"Let's pretend I'm Katriel," Velvel puts in, hopping around on his short legs. "Even if only for laughs."

"Long live Katriel" Itzik roars.

"Woe unto us," Zadok laments. "We're blaspheming! Here! At the holiest place in the world! God have mercy on us!"

"Where is Katriel?" says the blind beggar. "I want him to see me!"

"Who is Katriel?" Malka repeats, turning toward me.

She too has used the present tense. Is she teasing me? Punishing me? She surely knows where to strike. How am I to counter her blows? I could easily answer her question. I spent long hours, entire days with Katriel. I learned to know him so well I even wanted to change places with him. I envied him his vulnerability, his overwhelming need to love and be loved, his constant compulsion to magnify the human element in a world without humanity. I know that his son's death did not reconcile him to death. And for that too I envied him. Certainly he had suffered, but it was a suffering stripped of all humiliation for either himself or others.

"Katriel may still return," I say to his wife. "He is the one who will answer you. It is your duty to wait for him and his answers."

"I am waiting," she says. "I have been waiting for a long time."

A long time? Several weeks, several months. I still remember their last day together. He had arrived in time to teach his class. A student had suggested their listening to the morning news. The broadcast included some personal messages in code: mobilization orders for soldiers on leave, for those in the Reserves. Katriel had waited until the end of the broadcast; then he had put his notes back into his briefcase. Trying hard not to show his emotion, he had said: "It seems I'm needed elsewhere."

And after a pause: "Well, you will continue without me."

The students were so troubled that they had neglected to wish him good luck. He smiled when he recalled it later. Malka had known he was going to leave her. Had she suspected she would never see him again?

I watch her out of the corner of my eye. She lowers her glance as a sign of confession and helplessness, as if regretting, now that it is all over, that she had allowed her husband to die, or to survive as hero or beggar.

"I have learned to wait," she says with an air of defiance.

VII

A CLOCK struck two in the empty apartment next door: the doctor, meticulous and foresighted, must have wound his beloved clock before rejoining his unit.

Five more hours to go, Katriel thought. Time to put my papers in order, pack my things, put on the uniform, prepare for separation, store everything away in my mind. Then a jeep will stop in front of the house. Malka will overcome her sadness to offer me a parting sign of affection. Thus will begin for me a new journey toward the unknown.

"You'll see," he told his wife, "there will be no war. It's just a game. A round of poker, nothing more. Tomorrow I'll be back."

Malka had been silently staring at him since morning; unable to bear her look of disbelief, he had paced up and down the sunny room, stopping at times near the open window. In the street, a group of pedestrians had gathered around a boy on a bicycle who, one foot on the ground, was listening to his transistor radio. News bulletins followed one another, repeating one another: the government was deliberating, the opposition was getting increasingly impatient. The Western capitals were hoping to avert armed confrontation in spite of signs to the contrary. Statesmen and diplomats crossed oceans and frontiers, conferring and formulating ambiguous, meaningless declarations, promises and warnings. Foreign

press correspondents marveled at the calm prevailing
throughout the country, though mobilization had become
general.

"You see?" said Katriel. "No need to worry. They're preparing for war the better to avoid it."

The crowd dispersed, the boy got back on his bicycle and
sped away. In a moment the street became deserted again,
except for an elderly housewife who remained standing
there, forlorn and helpless. Katriel felt sorry for her: her
children, her sons-in-law, where would they be tomorrow?
But then, as though having regained her courage, she
abruptly brushed a mosquito from her face, retrieved her
basket from the sidewalk and was gone.

Katriel turned back to his wife: "Don't be sad, Malka."

"Why not?"

"To prove you have faith."

"In you?"

"In us."

"I do have faith and I'm not afraid of sadness."

"I am."

"I'll get used to it."

"Not me, not ever. I distrust habits, you know that."

Katriel felt her moving away from him into the past, or
perhaps into the future, and he wondered whether she
wanted to precede him there, or, on the contrary, to free
herself from him. Twenty years of living together, of shar-
ing, and what was she thinking about now? About their
happiness in the beginning when they had been able to accept it without compromising? About the fragility of human
ties? Two people defy evil and fiercely affirm the sanctity
of life; then destiny steps in and the whole edifice collapses.

"Please," Malka said anxiously, "don't say anything."

He wasn't going to say anything. There was nothing to

be said. At that very moment other men and other women, responding to the same need and stirred by the same forebodings, were facing each other and speaking as though for the last time: tomorrow the war would erase all words, all traces, all scars.

What if it had to be done all over again? Katriel wondered. He remembered what it had been like in his father's house, at school, at the yeshiva, in the army, where he had first met Malka. A memory: once while on leave he had gone to spend Shabbat with his father in Safed. In the morning, after services, they had studied together as usual, but Katriel had been unable to concentrate. Though blind, his father had noticed: "Is there something wrong, son?" Yes, the youth had confessed, something was wrong. Since donning his uniform, he could no longer accept the validity of a link between a Talmud two thousand years old and everyday life. And his father had smiled and explained very gently: "The link, my son, is you. You are the bridge between the Babylonian sages and the generations to come. Each man must consider himself responsible for both, each man contains all."

"Don't you think, Father, you are placing too heavy a burden on my shoulders?"

"Yes, perhaps. But you won't always have to bear it alone. You'll soon take a wife, you'll raise children, and they will transmit my name and yours so that one day the Messiah himself will hear their voice."

Shortly after, Katriel announced to his father that he had fallen in love. With whom? Her name was Malka, a name which pleased his father.

"Have you told her you love her?"

"No, Father."

"Why not?"

"I don't dare."

"Are you afraid she'll reject you?"

"Yes, Father."

"Your timidity is ill-founded, son. Loving is a privilege, greater even than being loved. Be proud of it, even if your love is not requited."

And Katriel remembered how, awkward and blushing, he had stood before the girl with the long black hair: "What I have to say to you must be said. Know that I love you, know also that even if you don't love me, I won't regret having told you, nor will I regret having loved you." She listened to him solemnly; then, without a word, without a smile, she drew him close and kissed him on the mouth: a kiss heavy with promise. Katriel freed himself from her embrace: "That's not enough, tell me you love me."

"Please," Malka had said, "don't say anything."

What was the use of looking back? If it had to be done all over again, Katriel thought, I would live my life the same way, with the same intensity. Despite the hard blows? Despite them. And Malka's silent suffering? I would try to tame it, transform it by giving it meaning and form. And the war? I would behave as if it did not exist. Of course, that would not be easy, it never had been. To Malka, thoughts of the future carried only visions of horror. An orphan, she had refused to bear children: she did not care to nourish Death. Yet she had let herself be persuaded by Katriel's father. And then there was Sasha. Sasha's innocent slumber. Sasha's growth, his affectionate gaiety. Sasha's intelligence, his precocious maturity. The child seemed to have decided to fight off the dark reign of fear all by himself. When Katriel came home at night, hardly had he opened the door when Sasha would jump into his arms and reel off the exploits of the day. Sometimes the child would whisper

97

into his ear: "You know, Mother is sad today, very sad, we must do something, but don't tell her I told you." Other times it was Katriel who sent the child to play with his mother, to amuse her, to cheer her up: "Be nice, very nice to her." Then came the day when the parents returned home alone and defeated.

They went on loving each other, struggling hard not to be consenting victims, not to deny themselves the possibility of hope. Each knew when the other pretended to have forgotten or feigned to be asleep. One night Malka began to sob: "I would like to understand, nothing more. I don't ask for much, just to understand." All Katriel could do was hold her close, closer than before. Understand what? And if we knew the truth, the whole truth, such as it reaches us, what would we make of it? That kind of truth is too pure and we are too weak to bear it: God alone is unafraid of His truth.

It was during a visit to his father that Katriel lost his self-control. According to the Talmud, his father reminded him, every soul possesses unlimited wisdom and knowledge which leave it when it reaches earth. Possibly these gifts come back to us after death. Too late to be of help. Katriel protested against the unfairness of such a scandalous game: "Thus it is in your presence, Father, that I often want to shout in order to exact a response."

"Why don't you?"

"I would hate to offend you."

"Me? You think of me, not about God?"

"Yes, Father."

"You sadden me. You are putting me between God and yourself."

They spent several hours studying. Then, in the middle of a passage, Katriel burst out: "We love You, God, we fear You, we crown You, we cling to You in spite of You, yet forgive me if I tell You my innermost thoughts, forgive me for telling You that You are cheating! You give us reason, but You are its limit and its mirror. You command us to be free, but on condition that we make You a gift of that freedom. You order us to love, but You give that love the taste of ashes. You bless us, and You take back Your blessing. Why are You doing all this, to prove what? What truth do You wish to teach us about whom?" And his father, aged and grief-stricken, answered: "It is not Him you must fight, but evil. And death. And the way to fight death is to create life."

Katriel did not agree. The death of a man is only the death of a man, but the death of a child is the death of innocence, the death of God in the heart of man. And he who does not drink deeply of this truth, who does not shout it from the rooftops, is a man devoid of heart, of God, he has never seen the misty eyes of a child expiring without a whimper, who dies before his parents and thus shows them the way. If I fall tomorrow, Katriel thought, I shall find my son again. Perhaps he will escort the Angel of Death, whom legend describes as made up of eyes, nothing but eyes: all he does is look, he kills by looking. If I fall tomorrow, I shall find my son's eyes again. And his mother will be alone at last.

"Malka . . ."

"No! Don't say anything!"

"Just this. Know that I love you. My love reaches toward you, even into your solitude. I do not wish to leave without saying it again."

Her lips trembled but not a single word emerged.

"Know too that I am thinking of Sasha while telling you this. Your sadness, like mine, has never interfered with my love for you."

99

Malka moistened her lips before murmuring: "You have pronounced his name. Now you can leave."

Suddenly there was such pain emanating from her whole being that it took Katriel's breath away.

"It seems so long ago," she continued in a barely audible voice. "Sometimes I wonder if it really happened, if Sasha was anything more than a dream, a desire. I needed to hear his name pronounced. Now you can leave."

One hour, two hours of silence. A car stopped in front of the house. Katriel thought: Now I must grab my bag, open the door, go downstairs and leave. And the road I take will lead me far from her, far from myself.

"I will come back," he said, kissing his wife's damp forehead. "There will be no war. There will be no victims. Everything will be all right, you'll see."

She forced herself to smile, but she did not go downstairs with him. Her hands clenched in her lap, she remained, somber and impassive, frozen to her chair, as though she had decided once and for all never to move again, never to speak again. Perhaps she was thinking of her son, of all sons torn from their fathers, of all fathers torn from life. Then night fell across the room. Malka welcomed it, rocking slowly back and forth in the chair and from time to time striking her head against the wall behind her with small, dull, desperate thuds.

Several days later I met Katriel. Malka never saw him again.

VIII

I REMEMBER the heat: stagnant under a bleak, opaque sky, it stifled the camp.

It had been a long, exhausting day. The afternoon was drawing to a close. Up since four in the morning, the battalion was waiting to move south. But departure orders were delayed. Why and for how long? Nobody knew. Counter-orders: unpack, set up camp again. The troops, ill-tempered, were openly grumbling. Some muttered: "What a way to start! If things keep going like this, we'll be beaten by the sun, not the enemy."

I had borrowed an old uniform from Gad, and was standing at the entrance of a tent. The soldiers of the third platoon lay stretched out on their cots, waiting for evening and the first gusts of cool air.

"Greetings," I said.

My future comrades didn't even look at me.

"The new sub-tenant, that's me. Where can I find Sergeant Yoav?"

The sergeant got up, grumbling: "You're the replacement for Asher?"

"Not exactly," I said, to avoid any possible misunderstanding.

"What's that you're saying?"

"I'm sorry, but I'm not replacing Asher, not really."

He examined me sullenly, which gave me the chance to do the same. Shoulders broad enough to support the tent's frame. A rough, striking face. Red all over: his bushy hair, his eyelashes, even his eyes.

"Let's start again, shall we? From the beginning. Asher broke his leg? Yes. I need a gunner? Yes. And you're standing here telling me it's not you?"

"Not really."

He became dangerously gentle: "Would you please be kind enough to explain yourself?"

"Gladly, Sergeant. You have an extra bed and I'm taking it. That's all. I should also inform you that I have never touched a gun in my entire life."

His face was something to behold. When a redhead blushes, chances are that blood is about to flow.

"Here, read this," I said, hoping to ward off a catastrophe.

I handed him my orders signed by Gad. They produced the desired effect:

"Why didn't you say so right off?"

Suddenly the others became interested:

"What does that piece of paper say?"

"Nothing much. David—that's his name—is doing us the honor of joining our unit until further notice."

Wavering between respect and suspicion, all participated in the interrogation I underwent on the spot. Age, family situation, residence, profession, political affiliations. My refusal to answer didn't make me a success.

Hostile voices:

"Who the hell does he think he is?"

"He's laughing at us."

"He's playing secret agent."

I stuck it out. So did they. The questions came fast from every side, without respite or restraint.

"Are you in Intelligence?"

"No."

"On active duty?"

"No."

"In the Reserves?"

"No."

"But you've been mobilized, haven't you?"

"No, gentlemen. Sorry."

"You were never in the army?"

"Never."

"How is that possible?"

"Never mind. It is possible, that's all that matters."

"But you're wearing a uniform, for God's sake!"

"Yes and no."

"He's pulling our leg!"

"And he has the nerve to ask for hospitality! Now we've really seen everything!"

Sheepishly, I had to clarify matters and confess that I was not really with the army, that I was not really mobilized, nor really a citizen.

"What are you then *really*?" one banterer inquired.

"A Jew," I said.

This simple but unexpected answer stopped them. But not for long. Somebody was quick to pick up the thread: "What will you be doing here? Anything special?"

"No idea. I think I'll be looking around."

Astonished by such insolence, they clicked their tongues and snapped their fingers in disapproval:

"Looking at whom?"

"At what?"

"No idea," I said, holding my ground. "Looking at you. At myself."

"Wonderful!" somebody exclaimed. "Tomorrow people will say: To be a Jew is to look."

Everyone roared with laughter, and I wished I could sink into the ground. My head buzzing and my cheeks on fire, I wanted to retrace my steps and clear out of the camp without even saying goodbye to Gad. But at that very moment a soldier emerged from the back of the group and extended his hand: "Welcome, David. My name is Katriel."

Tall, slim and graceful, endowed with natural poise, he seemed to have a special kind of influence over his comrades. Their attitude toward him was the kind one might have toward harmless madmen one is very fond of, for no particular reason.

"You mustn't laugh," he told them. "Looking and telling are neither easier nor less important than the rest."

He will testify for me, I thought even before I knew who he was. Obscurely I already sensed that he would play a role in my life, and perhaps in my death. For the moment his intervention saved me. The whole atmosphere changed. The sergeant showed me my bunk. I was initiated into the camp routine. Someone asked if I had eaten; I was not hungry. Another wanted to know if military rules applied to me too; I was not sure.

"What the hell!" the sergeant cut in. "You're here, make yourself at home. From now on, you're one of us. For better or worse."

Katriel intrigued me. I began to observe him. He suffered from insomnia. At night he would sometimes slip out quietly. Once I followed him outdoors. When he turned around, I was struck by the intensity of his gaze, in which light and shadow clashed. I noticed his lips; they were bleeding. In the silence which hovered over the sleeping camp, his presence took on another dimension. You may say I imagined it all. Possibly. Still he struck me as so strange that I turned around and, troubled, went back to our tent.

Through comrades who had known him before I had, I soon learned that in the beginning his behavior had been quite different. Awkward and disarmingly shy, he would blush and seem in agony each time he had to open his mouth to say yes, no, goodnight or thank you. Using gestures to express himself, he appeared to have only one wish: to render himself invisible. Having his name called out was an experience close to torture for him. He seemed as frightened of himself as of others. To become aware of his own existence would make him abashed, and he would lower his eyes, as if searching for a place to hide. Since he was considered a good sport otherwise, his anti-social character aroused only good-natured amusement. In order not to embarrass him, they would leave him alone in the evenings. Occasionally they would tease him, but never with malice.

The change in him occurred one evening when two men were having a bitter argument and almost came to blows. What about? The subject was unimportant. The country was under such tension that the slightest remark—about food, politics or the weather forecast—could stir up a tempest. The two were stopped, but the insults they had exchanged, hanging in the air, left the men ill-at-ease for hours. Conversation lagged. Here and there somebody made an attempt, formed a broken sentence, but would find no response. Finally Gdalia, a small, impetuous and jovial Yemenite, decided to make use of Katriel in an effort to raise everyone's spirits.

"See for yourself," Gdalia said to Katriel. "It's all your fault, it's your influence. Everyone imitates you. Because of you, everyone here is as silent as a grave."

He had hardly finished when a harsh voice, Katriel's, spoke up: "It's not my fault, at least I hope not. But if I'm wrong, I ask your forgiveness. And since you say nothing, I shall talk. I am not opposed to silence, you know that already. But I am opposed to silence which divides men. The kind of silence which tonight is creating hurt and bitterness among us."

Thunderstruck, the men jumped to their feet to see if it was really Katriel who had pronounced all these words without choking or fainting. Some shouted that they had witnessed a miracle.

Cheered by his success, Gdalia decided to exploit it further: "It's your fault, I tell you. You've cast a spell over them! By your silence you've robbed them of their power of speech!"

Poor Katriel. He was breathing with difficulty. His speech was like that of a sick man struggling to live and to speak: "You may be right. Everything is possible. After all, I am as responsible for my silence as you are for your words."

"Yes, yes," said Gdalia, unable to conceal his exuberance. "The fault lies with you, it's up to you to make amends. Recite a poem, deliver a sermon. Say no matter what, but say it!"

Katriel got up, lay down again, and started to speak: "Rabbi Nachman of Bratzlav compares the *yetzer hara*, the evil spirit, to the wicked magician who arouses people's envy and desire by holding up his tightly clenched fist to them. Succumbing to temptation, they force it open, certain they will discover there priceless treasures or secret documents, only to find it empty. However, I don't agree with Rabbi Nachman. No hand is ever really empty. The proof: even the magician's hand contained this very parable."

"I don't understand," said Gdalia, teasing him. "And if it's

a question of not understanding something, I prefer Spinoza."
He burst out laughing, but this time the others did not join
in.

Katriel looked at him sadly and continued in the same
humble manner, rubbing his temples as if to concentrate
better: "As a child when I was unable to understand what
my father taught me, it made me weep with rage and shame.
Rather than waste his time in explanations, he would console
me by saying: 'Whatever hides from your understanding,
love it all the more; you'll be rewarded and your love will
be returned to you.' I am still awaiting that reward, but it
no longer prevents me from loving stories."

Gdalia tried to interrupt but was ordered to be quiet.
Something in Katriel's voice succeeded in focusing his comrades' attention. He spoke softly, as though studying a sacred
text, as though trying to pierce the wall between word and
thought.

"I love stories," he said, "and it is thanks to my father
that I love them. Everything I know I learned from him.
He taught me to measure myself against my words and to
attune myself to their silence if not always to the truth they
conceal; he taught me how to listen. Do you know that it is
given to us to enrich a legend simply by listening to it? It
belongs as much to the listener as to the teller. You listen
to a tale, and all of a sudden it is no longer the same tale."

A distant memory brought a smile to his usually somber
face: "Do you realize that it is in our power to deepen the
source simply by moving toward it? And then drawing from
it? That too I learned from my father. I am just repeating
his words. But the silence within the words is my own."

He stopped. Entranced, the men did nothing, said nothing
which might break the spell. Even Gdalia, like a child filled
with wonder, remained quiet.

"I love silence," Katriel continued. "But beware: not all silences are pure. Or creative. Some are sterile, malignant. My father can distinguish between them with ease; I only with difficulty. There is the silence which preceded creation; and the one which accompanied the revelation on Mount Sinai. The first contains chaos and solitude, the second suggests presence, fervor, plenitude. I like the second. I like silence to have a history and be transmitted by it. My father and I . . . my wife and I . . . we can sit together whole evenings without exchanging a word, and yet, when we get up, we know we have told each other all there is to tell. If I have not succeeded with you, it's my own fault. I accept the blame and beg your forgiveness."

All of a sudden he realized that he was standing in the middle of the tent and making a speech. Covered with perspiration, he sighed apologetically and dashed toward the exit. Five pairs of arms grabbed him and hoisted him aloft in triumph. Gdalia, jovial and awake again, slapped his knees and laughed: "My God, he's drunk! That's the only explanation possible!"

"Don't say that," the sergeant protested. "Katriel never touches alcohol."

"I tell you he's been drinking. I ought to know. I discovered him, didn't I?"

Like an impresario hovering around his star, the little Yemenite boasted of Katriel's eccentricities.

"You want an explanation," he said, flushed with excitement, "you'll get one. It's simple. And logical at that. Until today Katriel neither spoke nor drank. Today he spoke; that means he drank too. That makes sense, doesn't it?"

In the general commotion, Katriel remained shy and forlorn. From then on, he was treated gently, almost spoiled by his comrades, who hoped to make him speak again. In vain. He responded only to excessive teasing. But Gdalia and his clique, afraid to hurt Katriel's feelings by overdoing things, chose to be patient. So I had to be patient too. Two days and two nights went by before my curiosity was satisfied.

LIKE everywhere else, conversation inside the camp centered on war: would it take place? Yes or no. Some dreaded it despite everything, others hoped for it despite everything. Time worked for the other side. A conflagration seemed imminent, inevitable. Should we take the initiative, or procrastinate? Pseudo-diplomats and instant strategists abounded: we should do this, say that. But all agreed on the outcome: we would win for lack of alternative. We had to win. The enemy could afford losing once, three times, ten times. For us, no victory would be final, while any defeat would be the last.

The danger grew sharper and sharper, with the vise tightening day by day, hour by hour. The tension had long since reached the breaking point. Determined to give diplomacy its chance, the government appealed to its friends for support. The enemy saw in that a proof of weakness. What should be done? Message from Paris: above all, do not fire the first bullet. Request from Washington: above all, be patient, keep us informed. Warning from Moscow: the enemies of our friends are our enemies or will become so. The Vatican, faithful to its principles, kept silent.

To the hundreds of journalists converging from the four corners of the earth, the country presented an unfamiliar face, confident but grim. Old men drove old taxis retrieved from the junkyard. Schoolchildren distributed mail, dug trenches and antiaircraft shelters, replacing adults in offices and in the fields. Few automobiles on the roads. Cafés and hotels deserted. Telegrams pouring in from relatives and strangers: Send us your children. Polite but categorical refusal: Jewish children will be protected and saved right here—or nowhere.

In expectation of an event, of the decisive test, under the eye of destiny, people conversed in hushed voices at home and in public places. Complete strangers spoke to and assisted one another. No panic in food stores. No pushing or shoving while standing in line. No rush for clothing. No flare-up of tempers while waiting for the bus. Never had people been so friendly to one another and to foreigners. Their personal anguish conferred dignity on them. One French correspondent wrote: "I am ashamed to appear outside in civilian clothes." Another journalist went even further: "I am ashamed not to be a Jew," he stated.

Meanwhile the enemy was openly preparing to attack. Former adversaries and ancient blood rivals concluded pacts and alliances, embraced before cameras, and placed their armies under joint command. The Soviet Union dispatched technicians and equipment. China promised the moral support of its masses, Algeria pledged planes and experts, Kuwait an armored division. In Arab capitals delirious mobs seethed with excitement and acclaimed the future heroes of the holy war, the total war. Orators invited Jewish women to make themselves beautiful in order to welcome the conquerors, who had clear and simple orders: burn the cities, raze the kibbutzim, slaughter all combatants, and drown the people of hope in an ocean of blood and fire. Words? Yes, words. Words which evoke laughter and fear. Words which haunt the cemeteries of Europe.

"And the world would stand by and let it happen?"

"Why not? It wouldn't be the first time."

"And what about the United Nations?"

"Delegates will make speeches. As usual."

"And our friends?"

"They'll make speeches too. But they'll weep on our graves."

The night I had arrived at camp, a discussion of this kind was producing bitter divisions among Yoav's men. I shuddered: the past held us in its clutches. Was that good or bad? The future would tell, and the war. One more war. The last. They always say that. Let us fight so as to fight no more. Let us kill so as to conquer death. Who knows, perhaps Cain himself aspired to be not just the first murderer in history but the last as well. One day the tale of this war will be told, and we will know it was not the last.

"If history repeats itself, I'll save the last bullet for myself. I have no desire to live as part of a society which refuses me the right to live."

The voice of Shimon. The sad voice, the clear determination of a former ghetto fighter.

"No! I don't agree. The right to live is something nobody can give me or deny me! That right I claim for myself and I won't allow anyone to challenge it!"

The anger of Yoav, the sabra, a young soldier from a Galilee kibbutz. Who says nothing has changed since the holocaust? We have changed.

"Tears, petitions, appeals to conscience, prayers, pressures are outdated," said Yoav. "It's high time to realize that. God doesn't love us, and neither does the world. Too bad. It's no longer our problem, but theirs. From now on, they will not count in our calculations. We shall ignore them. I couldn't care less what they say or don't say, what they think or don't think, what they approve or disapprove. Their judgment is no concern of mine. We alone shall decide what strategy to follow, whom to fight and when to stop. I don't give a damn any more whether humanity has a conscience or not. It never had any, that's what I think. I think all the grandiloquent talk about humanity's soul and conscience was invented by persecuted Jews as shield or alibi. So they wouldn't have to fight."

"Don't say that."

"Yes, Shimon. I will say it. Many persecuted Jews let themselves be massacred, like saints perhaps, but not like men."

"You are insulting the victims, the martyrs."

"If I have to insult them in order to survive, well then, I shall! They should have risen up in fury, they should have revolted, even if it meant setting fire to all of Europe, to the entire universe."

"Don't talk like that," Shimon implored. "By going to their death, the victims showed the world that it judged itself unworthy of either salvation or destruction; no living person has the right to hold that against them."

On the cot nearby, Katriel, his hands clasped behind his neck, was pursuing a private dream. Gdalia, for whom the holocaust sounded like part of some ancient mythology, kept out of the discussion. Shimon got up, hesitated a moment and went out. Yoav put out the cigarette he had just lit and followed him. Ephraim, the oldest and most pious of the group, groaned: "For how long, O Lord? And why?"

Katriel started to answer, but changed his mind.

Why and for how long? An innocent, childlike question that other Ephraims throughout the generations have never stopped asking. The Romans and the enemies of the Romans, the Christians and the enemies of the Christians, the Moslems and the mortal enemies of Islam: Ephraim was everyone's favorite target. They scoffed at him, they tortured him in the name of love for both man and God, they accused him in turn of poverty and wealth, ignorance and intelligence, loyalty and treason, weakness and strength, heresy and fanaticism; they killed him for the glory of days to come and others to forget, to avenge the past, both his and theirs. And each time he would whisper or shout: "For how long and why? Why us, why always us? What have we done to civilization that it is bent on rejecting us so often and with such ease? Why does mankind deem its existence incompatible with ours? For twenty centuries the names of executioners and victims have changed as circumstances and alleged pretexts have changed. But the question has remained the same and is more burning today than ever."

A memory: the ninth day of Av, in the dwelling of my Master, Kalman the Kabbalist, whose voice is unusually sad. We are sitting on the ground, lamenting the destruction of the Temple and studying texts of Jewish martyrology: tales and incantations of heartrending beauty. The Crusades, the autos-da-fé, the pillaging, the desecrations, the pogroms, the manhunts: all the Jewish tears gathered together and transformed into a song deeper than any abyss. I question my Master: "I can conceive of God's wanting to punish us for reasons that are His and not necessarily ours; but why do entire nations, so many nations, aspire to become His whip, His sword?" And my Master, his body emaciated by fasting, answers while looking at the burning candles: "The Jews are God's memory and the heart of mankind. We do not always know this, but the others do, and that is why they treat us with suspicion and cruelty. Memory frightens them. Through us they are linked to the beginning and the end. By eliminating us they hope to gain immortality. But in truth, it is not given to us to die, not even if we wanted to. Why? Perhaps because the heart, by its nature, by its vocation too, cannot but question memory. We cannot die, because we are the question."

In the tent nearby a radio was going full blast. Final broadcast of the day. Nothing new. Boastful blustering, swaggering ultimatums from the enemy. Neutrality, well-intended or not, on the part of this or that enlightened leader in Europe or Asia. In New York, in its glass palace on the East River, the United Nations Security Council, in urgent session, reconfirmed its powerlessness with great eloquence. Confronted by a hundred million Arabs, Israel emerged as the most solitary of nations.

Except that from this point on, shocked by Arab exhortations to genocide, public opinion in the free world raised the voice of its conscience. Even the Left took a stand against Moscow. The Communist Party, in many countries, was shaken up, split. The outrage provoked by Arab arrogance proved that Israel was not without friends.

Moreover, the entire Jewish people offered its unconditional support to the Jewish state and became its most faithful ally. In a show of solidarity of unprecedented intensity, a groundswell of amazing force rose up in the dispersed communities. Overnight the movement turned into a tidal wave involving Jews everywhere, in all imaginable areas and manners. Meeting night and day, action groups and coordinating bodies organized street demonstrations, rallies, petitions and mail campaigns. Funds and volunteers were mobilized on a massive scale. Never had this people been so united, never had it known such fervor. A former European cabinet minister proclaimed his shame at being the citizen of a country whose hypocritical policies condemned Israel to perish. A famed sociologist wrote that the disappearance of the Jewish state would rob him of all desire and strength to go on living. Intellectuals openly reclaimed the Jewish identity which they had formerly repudiated as an irritating contradiction. Assimilated Jews of long standing found themselves relieved of their complexes, sectarian Jews of their fanaticism. Writers and artists, hungry students and prosperous merchants, dreamers and realists, believers and atheists, rebels with and without causes, all found themselves concerned and in the same camp, carried by the same wave. All of a sudden each was responsible for the collective survival of all, each felt marked, singled out. A renowned violinist canceled his recitals and flew to Lydda, stating: "Our enemies claim they will exterminate two and a half million Jews, well then, let them add one more." The young, by the thousands, volunteered to go and fight, or at least to be there and help those who manned the front-line positions. From the depths of Mississippi, a businessman telephoned the Israel Consulate in New York: "I have lived all my life in shame of being Jewish. I want you to know I am no longer ashamed, I shall no longer hide. Today my children will be told who I am, who they are." A European banker proposed that all Jews adopt Israeli nationality in addition to their own. A great scholar went further: "If my government forces me to choose, painful as it may be, I shall opt for my threatened people."

I understood then that in time of trial man is more than himself, he represents more than his own person. When his roots are at stake, he becomes the sum of his experiences, given or acquired, a combination of intertwined destinies, a subterranean network of friendships and alliances. He becomes conscience. The illusions and the remorse, the shadows and those deprived of their shadows who have peopled his nights, they all are with him, within him, doing what he does, going where he goes, pushing him to commitment, to defiance. His love and concern are focused on that immense yet fragile chain, as though he were its final link. Spectator, he turns witness. Visionary, he now becomes all those characters to whom, long ago, he imparted a heartbeat, a glimmer of life.

On this level, the awakening seemed mystical. Haunted by the holocaust, the people of Israel and the State of Israel again had but a single memory, a single heart, and that heart vibrated with pride, strong in its fervor, surprised at its own fire: it was their first victory, and innumerable tales about it reached our camp through newspapers and radio.

In Safed, a rabbi whose intolerance in religious matters was well known, permitted his disciples to dig trenches on Shabbat. "To abandon man is more serious a sin than to abandon God," he told them. "The Torah of Israel depends on the existence of Israel. If the Almighty turns His back on His people, is that any reason for us to do likewise? I say no. I say that without Israel, the Shabbat will lose its sanctity. We shall therefore sacrifice the Shabbat to save our people."

Elsewhere, a *tzaddik* locked himself up in his study, and addressed his plea to God: "I have never questioned Your justice, Your mercy, though their ways have often confounded me. I have submitted to everything, accepted everything, not with resignation but with love and gratitude. I have accepted punishments, absurdities, slaughters, I have even let pass under silence the death of one million children. In the shadow of the holocaust's unbearable mystery, I have strangled the outcry, the anger, the desire to be finished with You and myself once and for all. I have chosen prayer, devotion. I have tried to transform into song the dagger You have so often plunged into my submissive heart. I did not strike my head against the wall, I did not tear my eyes out so as to see no more, nor my tongue so as to speak no more. I told myself: It is easy to die for You, easier than to live with You, for You, in this universe both blessed and cursed, in which malediction, like everything else, bears Your seal. I invented reasons, causes for rejoicing, to create a link to You and also to myself. But . . ."

Despite his resolve to hold back his tears, he felt them flowing through his hands. He let them flow. "But that's all over," he continued with redoubled strength. "Do You hear? It's all over, I tell You. I cannot go on. If this time again You desert Your people, if this time again You permit the slaughterer to murder Your children and besmirch their allegiance to the covenant, if this time You let Your promise become mockery, then know, O Master of all that breathes, know that You no longer deserve Your people's love and their passion to sanctify You, to justify You toward and against all, toward and against Yourself; if this time again the survivors are massacred and their deaths held up to ridicule, know that I shall resign my chair and my functions as guide, I shall fall to the ground, my forehead covered with ashes, and I shall weep as I have never wept in my life, and before dying I shall shout as no victim has ever shouted, and know that each of my tears and each of my shouts will tarnish your glory, each of my gestures will negate You and will negate me as You have negated me, as You will have negated Your servants in their dazzling and ephemeral truth."

Breathless and broken, the *tzaddik* laid his head, suddenly grown too heavy, on the table, as if to hide.

And this is what happened in the Ukraine.

Never had Kiev's only synagogue seen such a crowd. Two thousand persons. And most surprising of all: many young faces in the congregation. Ordinarily, the chief informer, a man called Yonah Goner, was in charge of keeping the youth away from worship. Surly, unpleasant, ill-tempered, he managed to suppress even the smallest efforts aimed at transmitting anything Jewish to the younger generation. As president of the synagogue, he ran it like a prison warden. Older people who regularly came to services trembled before him. He was capable of the worst.

But that evening the young arrived before he did and they were too numerous to be ordered out. He grasped the meaning of their presence immediately: to show solidarity with their brothers far away. The old men also understood. They radiated pride and happiness. Whispering, they took counsel and decided to strike a great blow. When Yonah Goner signaled the cantor to begin services, three of the elders stood up and ordered him to remain seated. Then the oldest of the three, looking straight into the president's eyes, stated firmly for all to hear: "As long as an informer is present, we are not permitted to pray together."

"What?" Goner exclaimed. "What's that you're saying?"

The spokesman repeated his statement, explaining that it was based on Halakhah, or Talmudic law.

"Have you gone mad?" Goner bellowed at the top of his voice. "Irresponsible, that's what you are! You think you are free to do as you please? This call to disorder and insubordination may prove very costly!"

"We know."

"You'll pay for this."

"Gladly, Comrade President."

"Cantor! Begin the service! Don't listen to these fools! Go ahead, that's an order!"

The cantor did not move. Crimson, in a paroxysm of rage, Goner dismissed him on the spot, and invited other worshippers to take his place. No one got up.

"Of course, you can denounce us and be avenged," said

the spokesman. "We are old, we haven't much left to lose. We are ready for anything." Abruptly he raised his voice: "From now on, we shall be free Jews at least in our relations with you. It is, therefore, as a free man that I demand your resignation. Go home so that we, as a congregation, may turn our thoughts toward meditation and prayer."

In the synagogue, two thousand spectators held their breath. It took the young a moment to understand what had taken place before their eyes. Their elders were smiling and nudging one another, and everyone felt light-hearted and free.

"No!" Goner shouted. "I won't resign! I won't go away!"

"In that case," said the spokesman, "there will be no services this evening."

The scene repeated itself several times. The Jews of Kiev would come to the synagogue, and so would Goner. They would remain there silently for an hour or two. But no services were held. No Kaddish was said, no blessing recited. Finally, unable to bear the shame, Goner yielded and left. So the cantor began officiating again, and the Baal Koreh read the Torah aloud from the pulpit.

And the Jews of Kiev, still proud of their adventure, will tell you to this very day: "Israel's war? We had a share in it."

Because, in fact, all Jews everywhere took part in it, each in his own fashion. And we, in our camp, were aware of their participation. Playing the role of messengers, lecturers traveled from unit to unit, bringing us new courage with their reports of a seemingly boundless collective involvement. We were filled with wonder as we listened and bombarded them with questions: What is the attitude of such and such a statesman, industrialist, novelist? Our hopes rose with each answer. Yes, miracles were not only needed and necessary, they were also possible: yes, ours was the power to break and overcome the millennial Jewish solitude. The more stories our guests told, the more we exhorted them to continue. They had to tell us everything, we wanted them to omit nothing.

IX

YES, those were memorable days, historic days we were living. That much was clear, that much was tangible. Not being fond of big words, we did not bother enunciating them. What use were fancy phrases? We had other things to worry about. We knew this armed watch could not, would not last forever. The gods of war, gone mad, had already dragged us to the edge of the precipice. At any moment events transforming the face of the world could be set in motion: we were taking part in that metamorphosis.

As for me, I had already completed my own. I, who considered myself a die-hard rebel against communal life, against military discipline, quickly adapted myself to both. Renouncing my privileges and my taste for solitude and the unexpected, I became entrenched in the collective structure of the camp. I got up and went to bed at fixed hours, and like everyone else I cursed the heat and the drills, the monotony and the uncertainty; and I, who resent anything sentimental, was moved when in late afternoon villagers would bring us cakes, sweets, wine and the latest magazines.

I sought out Katriel's company. His behavior excited my imagination. He listened well and had, like me, a capacity for living the lives of others. Except that, unlike me, he did not rebel. He became one with whoever spoke to him.

His belief in people impressed me. He never doubted anyone's word. In his view, all human beings possess a spark of truth which disperses darkness in spite of them. "What about liars?" we would ask. "Oh, liars think they're witty," was his answer. "Most of them lie just to squander their share of truth—and fail."

Our first real conversation took place one Saturday when the camp was besieged by visiting women and children. I had remained in our tent. So had Katriel.

"It's stupid of me," he said, "but I find these family reunions painful, almost destructive." He hesitated. "I ought to envy you. You are alone. You can live or die without involving anyone else. You depend on no one, and no one depends on you."

"How about you?"

"I am committed."

"So am I," I said.

It was true. I would never be free of the friends I had once cherished, the women I had loved, now dead or vanished.

"You'll think it's funny," I said after a while. "But lately it seems to me I should be the one to be envious."

"Of me?"

"No, not just of you."

It was true. I envied our companions their attachments and problems. Also their fear of death. Nothing is so depressing as a road without end.

"This is quite stupid," said Katriel. "We are practically strangers and yet we envy each other. As if that served any purpose."

That same evening, on his own, he told us a disturbing parable. It went like this:

One day a man leaves his home, his native village where

time does not exist, and goes off in search of a rainbow, an adventure. He heads toward the faraway and magic city. Evening falls and he is caught in the midst of a forest. He selects a tree with thick foliage under which to spend the night, sheltered from wind and rain and thieves. Before falling asleep he removes his shoes and places them nearby, pointed in the direction of the road he is to follow in the morning. Could he foresee that around midnight, in order to confuse him, punish or save him, a practical joker would turn his shoes around, pointing them back toward his village? At dawn he arises, thanks God for giving back his sight and soul to him, and suspecting nothing, continues merrily on his way. From a hilltop, he sees at last the mysterious, promised city. He had imagined it larger, different. Seen from nearby, it seems curiously familiar: the river, the gardens, the crossroads are exactly like those in his hometown. Moreover, he thinks he can recognize each building and guess who lives there. To the right: the inn and its drunkards, dirty not because they like dirt, but because they distrust water. Farther on: the city hall, with its faded tricolored flag hanging down from its pole like the head of a tired old horse. To the left: the police station, serving as buffer between the grocer and the butcher, at loggerheads more as a matter of tradition than of necessity. Behind the municipal theater: the market, where the visitor knows what each housewife will buy, at what cost, and from which farmer. Feeling more surprised than disappointed, our traveler thinks: "Well now, they've told me lies. The big city has nothing to boast about, it holds no secrets, maybe it doesn't even exist, only my village exists, it is its image I see reflected in the world." From that moment on, nothing astonishes him. He knows that turning the next corner, past the shoemaker's, he will find himself in front of a house just like his own. Yes, the door is slightly ajar. "Odd, the lock needs fixing, just like at home." From inside, a voice invites him to enter: "You must be hungry, come and eat." He could swear it is his wife's bossy, whining voice. It is enough to drive him mad, but being hungry, he might just as well obey and not make a fuss. Besides, he has always obeyed his wife. He crosses the kitchen and enters the living room with its windows facing a court bordered with greenery. He sits down at the table. The children smile at him, and he is overwhelmed by sadness. The smallest one clutches at his knees, plays with his beard and whispers in his ear: "You'll stay with us, won't you? You won't leave us, will you?" Because he does not want to disappoint the child and because he feels that it's no use, he is trapped, the stranger caresses the child's golden hair and ends up promising him everything.

Katriel stopped short, reflecting as if to make sure how the tale continued. Then he repeated the last words: "Yes, he ends up promising him everything."

"And then?" I asked, leaning forward to see him better.

"Then nothing."

Something in his parable disturbed me. It sounded familiar. The way it reverberated in me was not new.

"Yes, he kept his promise," Katriel continued. "He never returned to his village. Death went looking for him there, but did not find him."

And staring at an invisible point in space, he began nodding his head as if saying yes-yes to the child, yes-yes to the stranger, and perhaps even to death.

"That story of yours doesn't make any sense," someone objected. "On arriving in his 'new' home, your traveler would logically have had to come across his double."

124

"You don't understand philosophy," Gdalia snickered. "What Katriel means to say is that the double had also gone off on a spree . . ."

"Looking for a wanderer perhaps?"

"Or for death?"

"You're all boring us stiff," said Gdalia, Katriel's self-appointed protector.

Yes, I had heard that story before, I was thinking. When, where and from whom? I did not remember, and that annoyed me as I was annoyed each time my mind, in a feverish outburst, invented for itself insuperable obstacles. This traveler, with his escapes and failures, was no stranger to me. And so, prompted by a confused impulse, I vented my anger on Katriel.

"I don't like your parable," I said to provoke him.

"Because you recognize yourself in it?" said Gdalia, sitting up on his cot.

Heedless of the interruption, I continued: "Your parable ignores the real wife, the real children, who, abandoned in their tiny village, wait in vain for the traveler's return. Their fate concerns me as much as his; their suffering is as important as his quest."

I had expressed myself with passion. All eyes were focused on me in reproach and perplexity, as though I were guilty of some terrible offense. In the oncoming twilight, I saw Yoav scowling, wondering what on earth could have upset me so. In truth, I wondered myself.

"Please continue," said Katriel with humility.

I paused a moment, but was unable to control either my voice or my words: "I also dislike your main character. He lies. As a result, he makes you lie. It is inconceivable to me that a man could shed his 'I' as he might an attachment or a memory. That 'I' sticks to him and belongs to him and only to him; it is he. One does not exchange one's 'I' for another, even a more refined or truer one. Your character can kill his 'I' by letting himself be killed, which is not easy either; but he can certainly not shake it off along the way. The 'I' is comparable to death. Your traveler can live and even die for you, but not in your place."

Why had I lost my temper? Why had I turned a simple tale into a metaphysical argument not to my liking? Katriel had aroused in me an animosity which for the moment I could neither justify nor clarify. Had he not come to my defense? Had I not found in him the human qualities I usually value in another? Had I not sensed an ally in him? Was it his fault if his parable had set off an alarm inside me?

"You may be right," Katriel answered in a hurt but gentle voice. "I have no authority to speak in his place or in his name. It may be his fate to live a lie and submit to it freely and deliberately, out of excess or lack of pride. Perhaps all he wants is to lie to death so he may finally be allowed to die. Yes, I think we should leave him the last word since he was denied the first."

He smiled: "But a tale is only a tale after all, isn't it? It is made to be lived and then passed on; the rest, David, is not up to us."

He was waiting for me to refute his words, but the desire to argue had left me. Considering the debate closed, Gdalia, now our moderator, declared Katriel the winner.

Someone parted the canvas folds of the tent. I saw the sky deepen, turn gray, gather the first shapeless shadows. The heat lifted. We could breathe. In the distance, a sergeant was shouting. A jeep sped by, raising a cloud of dust. Two officers were calling to each other across the tents. Noises of chains being lifted and pulled. A voice, nearby, ordering a blackout. Heaven and earth split asunder so as to make way for the twilight, heavy with foreboding. The camp was withdrawing into itself, its anguish and its secrets. Suddenly I felt myself shivering. I did not understand why. When I finally did, it was late, too late.

X

I FELT oppressed and could not fall asleep. Nor think clearly. A migraine was starting in my temples, swelling my eyes, dwarfing my face. To escape the pain, my body pulled in all directions at once. At first I resisted, and the trembling that followed shook me all the more. Then I let myself float. Through the mist I watched the events and people of preceding days disintegrate in the distance. Images and symbols disengaged themselves from me; I was shrinking away under my own eyes. Friends and strangers, in a blur, pointed fingers at me, muttering unintelligible sounds. Years ago, in a hospital, before losing consciousness during surgery, I had experienced the same sensation of impotence, of loss. I was sinking. A slow, agonizing fall. And as I was falling, I felt a chasm opening up beneath me. The more I wanted to hold on to what I was, the more I was becoming another. Where was I?

I sat up, pulled myself together. All was calm in the tent. Through the slit in the canvas the silvery night appeared for a brief moment, rested lightly on Katriel's forehead, then withdrew. I stretched out again. The pain was growing more intense, a fiery whip thrashing my brain. Take a sedative, a sleeping pill? Light a match, find the medication, the water container: too complicated. The slightest effort seemed a great challenge. Better let myself grow numb.

Inertia was the easy way out. And then, I knew from experience that once the first attack was over, it would be possible to hide inside the pain itself.

With clenched fists I waited for the first wave and submitted to its assault. Then my anxiety welled up again, constricting my chest, my throat, my entire being. Deep down in my consciousness I had already guessed that it stemmed not from anything that happened, but from the tale I had just heard. It was an ancient anxiety, linked to other landscapes, other encounters. How could I explore its meaning and origin? Searching in my memory, I began to lose its threads. Faces, names, objects: adrift in time, they surged and turned and vanished in a whirl, only to emerge again, unchanged but multiplied. Bathed in unearthly white light, they were all within reach of my hand, my glance, but which one should I grab, which one choose? There were too many, too interwoven and all forgotten. No single episode, no single expression held me long enough to reveal a direction, an opening. Aborted dreams, suppressed revolts, burst passions, burnt out too soon, too late: a fragment of hope, an attempted project, an adventure removed from reality. A sick man prepares to disclose his secret and dies without speaking; a grandmother, a black shawl over her head, absent-mindedly caresses an invisible orphan. And there, in the midst of these beings without consistency, without future, there in the very center of phantasmagoria sits a figure, peaceful and motionless, a woman who in a previous existence may have been mine, perhaps still is. She smiles at me, from far away as always, from the other side of a river. Are you well? — Yes, I am well. — Whom are you looking for? — You. — You mustn't. — I know, she says. I mustn't. Nor you. You too must stop looking. — I have no choice, I tell her. What else can I do? — She tilts her head gracefully, resigned to waiting. A lump in my throat, I turn away to follow other clues, other traps, deeply buried but intact. Attempts at living in Paris, at faith in Williamsburg, at friendship in Tangier. A mountain cave, a prison cell. I stumble over an executioner here, a victim there, and beneath their features I find my masks again. And always that same anguish, ever the same, bursting in my limbs, flowing through my veins. Now it carries me back into my childhood, back to my native town, to the secret subterranean kingdom where the beginning has a voice, throbbing and melancholy. — A woman—my mother—calls to me: You are so pale, you are not sick, I hope? — No, Mother. I'm well. — You seem preoccupied. You're not without friends, I hope? — I've lost my friends, Mother. I'm looking for them. — You've done well to return; they are here. — But that's not all. I'm also looking for a story, a parable. — You've done well to return, my son. All parables, all stories are here. — Here? Where? — At home, my son. Only, there is no more home, the asylum with its madmen is all that remains. I run away. I rush over to my grandfather's: Help me! The old man answers: Too late. I run to Kalman the Kabbalist: too late. My Master has forgotten his prayers, my grandfather his tales. Outside, in the street, I stop a beggar who once was fond of me: Save me! — Too late, he says, laughing. — Too late even to laugh? — Even to laugh! — My head spinning, I accost, one by one, all the people who once occupied a place in my life and who, having been contaminated by my fever, are now wreaking havoc in my wavering mind. Penitents, messengers, wandering preachers: each had burdened me, one with his blessing, another with his silent song. One had revealed to me the destiny of the man who, having fled from himself, was condemned to mark time forever. And, at the end, the storyteller had added:

"One day this tale will be told to you, and then . . ." Then, what?

I jumped: was that Katriel's voice? I held my breath and listened. Nothing. If Katriel had awakened, he gave no sign. Spying on him like this made me feel guilty. Yet I saw nothing. All I heard was the wind, outside, gliding across the canvas, beneath a starlit glacier.

I got up and went out on tiptoe. The light outside had a dreamlike quality. The cold revived me. A shiver ran down my spine. How beautiful it is, I thought. Do you know, Malka? The woman resembled you. Do you know how poignant night is when the beast, having selected his prey, tenses before devouring it? Do you know how excruciatingly beautiful the night is, flowing toward the desert like a river, flowing like the blood in the veins of a dying heart? Tomorrow, I thought, tomorrow perhaps all this beauty will end up in butchery.

Suddenly there was a presence behind me, I felt eyes looking at me.

"I can't sleep," said Katriel.

At that moment I was not sure whether he was alive or whether he too was part of my past.

"I'm not sleepy," he continued. "Anyway, I don't need much sleep."

His hands in his pockets, his head sunk into his shoulders, he scanned the horizon as if he too was seeking something, or someone, and finding nothing, was content to breathe in the fresh air.

"Are you angry?" he asked. "I had no intention of hurting you."

I said nothing.

"I'd like to talk to you," he said after a silence. "Who knows if there'll ever be another chance."

131

Still unsure whether it was Katriel I was seeing and hearing, I did not reply. He took it as a sign of hostility.

"Forgive me," he said and sighed. "I didn't mean to intrude. I'm going back to try and get some sleep."

"Wait a minute. Come closer."

He hesitated but obeyed.

"Where did you get that tale of the traveler?"

"From my father."

"Do I know him?"

"I don't believe so."

"And your father? Is it possible he knows me?"

"Not likely. He is blind."

My father had good eyes, I thought, withdrawing again. Or rather, no, he was blind too. But in a different way. The world and the men in it were not quite as he saw them.

"That tale," I said, "I've heard it before."

"It's possible."

"I'm positive."

Katriel felt the need to explain: "My father's tales are not original, you know. They don't always belong to him alone. Frequently they are merely reflections of those which other men are living through."

Then, in a flash of lucidity, I perceived the solution to the mystery. Somewhere in my childhood a wild-eyed beggar, his palms outstretched, had asked me for some wine and bread for Shabbat. I had invited him to our table, but he had refused: "Men frighten me, their tales put me in jeopardy. Remember, child, remember that the day someone tells you your life, you will not have much longer to live."

Suddenly I understood that Katriel's traveler might have been myself. Disguised as a stranger, I might have been living beside women who were mistaking me for someone else. "I" had remained over there, in the kingdom of night, a prisoner of the dead. The living person I was, the one I thought myself to be, had been living a lie; I was nothing more than an echo of voices long since extinguished, nothing more than a shadow stumbling against other shadows whom I was cheating and betraying day after day, as I forged ahead. I thought I was living my own life, I was only inventing it. I thought I had escaped the ghosts, I was only extending their power. And now it was too late to retrace my steps.

I pushed my mind to its limits. I did not want it to stop now. Faster, farther: let it go to the end. Suppose I was the traveler and this tale my tale—what then? I saw the beggar again, I heard his warning. If indeed he had spoken the truth, then I owed it to him and to myself to take certain precautions, certain measures; I had no more time to lose.

What does one do when fighting one's disarray? I breathed as deeply as I could, I coughed and was afraid of the noises I produced. I let my hands fumble in my pockets, as though not knowing what I wanted them to find. Katriel's staring at me added to my confusion. Should I disclose the message that, unaware, he had just delivered to me? Confess that he had unwittingly made himself the instrument of death? I preferred to spare him.

"I don't know what the war has in store for us," I said. "But I offer you a pact: let us stay together. I will help you conquer fear and the enemy; in exchange, you will remember me as I am, as I will be. Don't try to understand. You'll understand later. And even if you don't understand, no matter. All I ask is that you watch me closely, listen to me carefully. Remain beside me. Always. Even in combat. Especially in combat. Try to inscribe in your memory my every gesture, my every word. Do you agree?"

"But . . ."

"No questions. Will you say yes?"

Bewildered, Katriel lost his composure. He opened his mouth, closed it again. Finally he mumbled: "I'd like to think it over."

"Time is running out."

"For whom? For us?"

"For peace."

"Who said so? Your friend Gad?"

"No, not he."

He shuddered. I thought: How vulnerable, how innocent is the face of a man at night, the face of a man whom you choose as your ally, your heir. Do you know, Malka, do you know how pure, how sad is the trembling of a man who, foreseeing his role as witness, suddenly glimpses the mutilation or end of a life other than his own? Do you know, Malka, how profoundly human and how wounded is the voice of a friend who senses, in you and in the night surrounding you, the shame inherent in survival?

"I wonder what my father would say about your offer," Katriel said, deep in thought.

"He would advise you to accept."

"For what reasons?"

"He has undoubtedly agreed to a similar pact."

"My father? A pact?"

"Exactly."

"With whom?"

"What difference does it make? Let's say with God."

"What in heaven's name would God have to do with such pacts?"

"Let's say He likes taking part in all pacts."

"But what would be His interest?"

"Let's say He also needs witnesses. In the beginning there was the word; the word is the tale of man; and man is the tale of God."

I expected him to cry out in protest against my blasphemy; he did not. He knew as well as I that what I had said was not blasphemy.

"I have one question," he said in a changed voice.

"Yes?"

"Who told you what our roles would be? Who told you that you won't get out of this? And that I will?"

"Our pact works both ways, Katriel. The one who survives will bear witness for the other."

"But you know nothing about me!"

"Nothing? Your questions, are they nothing? Your tales, are they nothing? The way you talk, the way you listen and watch, nothing? Your passion for mystery, for silence, nothing?"

"You mean that's all I am?"

"Those are elements, a few among others, many others. Together they make up what you are, each expressing a particular aspect. The fragments are signposts, keys. You yourself will supply me with the rest later."

"Later? When? And how will I go about it? I don't like words! They destroy what they aim to describe, they alter what they try to emphasize. By enveloping the truth, they end up taking its place."

"Perhaps you are lending too much importance to words. Tell yourself that they too are God's creation. Tell yourself that they possess an existence all their own. You prefer to feed truth with silence? Good. But you risk distorting it with contempt."

Uncertain, he shook his head several times. Better not press him further. He had not yet given me his consent, but I knew I would get it. I granted him a moment of reprieve to remove any feeling of constraint. Then I held out my hand: "Well, Katriel? Agreed?"

He let my hand hang in midair: "Why did you choose me?" he asked.

"I couldn't tell you. Because we are so different, you and I? Perhaps. Haven't you ever had the desire to be what you cannot be?"

"No, never."

"You see how different we are. I have. More than once."

"I don't think that's your only reason."

I had to break his last resistance: "True enough. There is another reason. Let's say I prefer making a gift of my tale to someone who would know how to tell it."

My reply should have made him smile, but his face remained grave and tense. Then he sighed as if interpreting a thought that had just crossed his mind. "Agreed," he said.

Whereupon he shook my hand with surprising force.

XI

"**D**ID he speak about me?" Malka asks.

"Very little."

Katriel had spoken to me mainly about his father, an obscure rabbi in Safed, who had no one on earth but his son. On grounds of health or as yeshiva student, Katriel could easily have obtained an army exemption or deferment as early as 1948. His father would not hear of it. What is more, he ordered Katriel to volunteer.

"But, Father, why not wait at least for my call-up papers?"

"Our people are in danger, and you, my son, would have the patience to wait?"

"But who will look after you?"

"Our people are rising up from the ashes, and you, son, worry about me?"

The rabbi made him sit down in front of him, and his voice was soft but fiery.

"Don't you understand that through you, son, with you, I too shall share in the holy task of renewal?"

"But, Father! What about my studies? Didn't you dedicate me to Torah and God?"

"You will go back to them afterwards."

"When?"

"Afterwards."

"And if I die?"

"God protects those who sanctify His name."

"Father, what if I die?"

The rabbi leaned forward as though to take full measure of the son he could not see. "Are you afraid?"

"Yes, Father."

"Afraid of suffering, afraid of dying?"

"Yes, Father, I'm afraid."

The rabbi sighed. "You still have a lot to learn, my son. What you should fear is to inflict evil, to cause death. To die for God and His commandments is nothing: our ancestors, the saints and the martyrs, did just that. But to kill for God, to cause blood to flow in His name, is serious and difficult. It is alien to us; it goes against our nature and tradition: that is what should frighten you."

"And he said nothing about me?" Malka asks.

"I told you. Very little. You met in the army. You never told him you loved him. He didn't hold that against you. He understood and saw it your way. When one loves, what need is there to say 'I love you'? Every gesture affirms it, so does every heartbeat. When one loves, one says it simply, naturally, by the way one walks, gets up or sits down; by the way one lowers one's eyes before the being one discovers anew and desires afresh at each moment. Isn't that true, Malka?"

"Yes, it's true."

"His description of your life together is correct?"

"Yes, absolutely correct."

"He also told me of Sasha's death. He loved the child very much, but he loved you even more. Did you know that, Malka?"

"No, I didn't know."

"He felt you were more fragile than Sasha, more threatened. He used to tell me: 'My wife needs me even more than my son did. And I need her.' You knew that, didn't you?"

"No, I didn't know."

"You liked to sing and be happy together. At night or on Shabbat he would take you in his arms and say: 'We have a son, he's handsome and happy; we have the right to express our joy.' And later, after the accident, he would take you with passion and despair, murmuring: 'We had a son, he's dead now, but we have no right to weep or indulge in sadness, we have no right to concede defeat.' He needed to know you were happy. Even later. Especially later. His faith in himself and in the future depended on you and your reactions to his efforts. You knew that, didn't you?"

"No, I didn't know," Malka sighs.

"What then did you know?" I ask angrily.

Across the dark main square one can hear the faint chanting of worshippers standing before the flickering candles, sounding at times like a song of the blind, at times like the frightened whisper of a traveler lost in mid-forest.

"I'm cold," Malka says.

I remove my jacket and wrap it around her shoulders. My fingers accidentally brush the nape of her neck and linger there. Impossible to pull them away. This is their place and has been since man's awakening to desire. I suddenly want to touch this woman as Katriel had touched her, speak to her as Katriel had spoken to her. My fingers feel her body responding to mine. Let whatever separates us be erased, let us become one and think of nothing else.

"I'm cold," Malka repeats, shivering.

I too am termbling, but not with cold. On the contrary, I am on fire. I am suffocating. And Katriel? I no longer wish to invoke his face and promise. I no longer remember whether Malka is his wife or mine. I am not even sure if David is David and not Katriel.

"Let's walk," I say, afraid of my next thought.

Malka nods assent. I help her to her feet. Velvel, envious and repulsive, sneers knowingly. Zadok disapprovingly lowers his eyes. My understanding blind friend Shlomo whispers to me between his teeth: "Go ahead, brother. The night is long, perhaps someone is waiting for you."

The madmen are convulsed with laughter, while the beggars hurl words of counsel and encouragement. The young pilot, already one of us, would like to join me in my dream.

We circle the square. Malka holds my hand and I am penetrated by her warmth. We sit down on the ground, in a remote corner at the foot of the Wall. Alone with Malka. Only stones and stars. And silence. Gone the feelings of oppression, shame and guilt. I am free and at peace with the present. And to think that this might not have happened to me at all. Or that it might have happened to someone other than me.

"Speak to me," Malka implores.

The new intimacy in her voice surely means something. I prefer not to think about it, not to see its meaning, not to let myself be carried away.

"Talk to you? About whom?"

"Anyone you like."

"Katriel?"

"It doesn't matter. About him. Yourself. Us. Anyone you like."

"How can I talk about him? He went away too soon, too quickly. Before me. Death did away with its own messenger."

"Don't talk about death. Please. Find something else. Anything else."

"I'm sorry. Katriel reminds me of death."

"Don't talk about him."

"As you please."

"Tell me about yourself."

"What would you like to know, Malka? That again death has played one of its tricks on me?"

"Don't talk about death," she says.

I think of Katriel, of Sasha. They are dead, but Malka wants me to play along with this make-believe. Had he lived, Sasha would now have reached the ungrateful age, the age of revolt, questioning systems and values, upsetting the established order. And one day he would have turned to his father and asked: "What right did you have to bring me into this world?"

"Your thoughts are frightening," says Malka. "They separate you from me, from us."

Over the years other women had begged me in the same way to speak or not to speak about past experiences, to think or not to think of them any more. Only the present and the future were of interest to them: plans to travel, to discover, to love, to live together, vows and promises to remain faithful to each other and to face and defy together anything that might oppose our chances, our very possibilities of being. We walked along the road side by side, and I knew I was alone again.

"Look, Malka . . ."

"Your way of looking is frightening."

"Look and you'll be reassured. Look at the mountain. It is moving, it is climbing the sky. Watch it rising higher and higher. Can you see it? The mountain is embracing the sky."

"I see no sky."

"And the mountain?"

"Yes, I see the mountain."

"Tell me what you see."

"The head of a man. Dark and heavy. Forbidding, untouchable. Anyone who approaches it, who tries to love it, must relinquish his freedom. That's why the mountain has taken over the sky."

Anxious again, shaking with fever, I wonder whom she is thinking of: me or Katriel? Sasha perhaps.

Her eyes half closed, she curls up against me and offers me her face, her trembling lips; she offers me her desire. How dare she? It is maddening. Could I have traveled so long a road only to fall into this trap? I bite my lips, tense my muscles: whatever the cost, I must resist. David owes it to Katriel and also to Malka, who is more than just Malka. Katriel, to me, is every friend I ever had and lost. Malka, to me, is every woman I ever desired, loved or gave up. And I, who am I? I have been racing from one labyrinth to the next for so long, provoking death so often and with such passion, that I no longer know why I am fleeing or why I am renouncing what is offered me.

"Come back," Malka says weakly.

Could it be Malka begging me to come back? Come back from where? To do what? To make love? Here? Now? What a strange place for love, what a strange place for the repudiation of love. But cannot the same be said of all times, all places, all situations? Is there anywhere a love untainted by betrayal? To love—does not the very verb imply an exclusion of the outside world with its living and dead? But if one says no to love, is one not also guilty of the same denial? There lies the trap: the yes and the no carry the same weight, open or shut the same gates to the same redemption. Are you listening, Katriel? And you, Malka, do you grasp the danger inherent in desire? And you, men and women who sit in judgment, do you understand now that love, no matter how personal or universal, is not a solution? And that outside of love there is no solution?

For I must tell you I could love this woman who is not mine, I could truly love her, joining my breath and hers, my waiting and hers, I might even succeed in saving her, in showing her a way, giving her the spark to transform her love into something less absurd, less inhuman. One word, one gesture would suffice. She would consent, I feel it. She would be grateful, I know it. And Katriel? We would learn how to push him back, how to forget him. Except that he would not forget us.

"Malka," I say to the woman, "Malka, this night does not belong to us, but I summon it and desire it dark and unending. I have nothing to give you but this night, so let it be my offering, the only one we both deserve."

And she answers: "What are you to me? A way of remembering, of waiting for absence to become blurred so that the bush and its flame may appear? No. A changing name to hide a face that stays forever open and identical? No, not that either. It's much more simple, more concrete: you are what I desire to possess always, so as to dispense with speech and memory. You are the moment of awareness thanks to which I am what I am: a woman who believes in love since she loves, who believes in freedom since she offers herself to you."

We talk, and our nervous, groping hands, like frightened children's, seek one another, knotting and intertwining. I want to laugh, to shout, but I am afraid to open my lips. I am afraid of Katriel, I am afraid of myself. There is in me such hunger for love, for forgiveness, that I think it will stay with me forever. In my delirious mind I see myself as I am, as I have been: I am the haggard traveler, wandering aimlessly, looking at men but taking nothing from them. I am the child refusing to be born, and Malka is the dying princess refusing to die. Together we run, run after the hallucinated nomad who, his mouth filled with blood, is fleeing the source, his own and ours, to abandon himself to the naked desert, haunted by the gods. As we run we call to him to come back: "You are too young to live or die away from men!" He does not hear us. I therefore ask the woman to cling to me, to hold me and cover me with her love. And I tell her: "In the world beyond worlds, men are vacillating, suffocating, rejecting love beyond love, good beyond good. They are blinded by the sun and numbed by its death. Exhausted, and in despair, they give up all ties and choose to become madmen or beggars; they choose death, absence or saintliness; they want nothing, nothing more than the friendly wink of one creature fulfilled, the softness of a generous and trusting hand, the glimmer of a distant lamp in a hospitable country. They are alone and dread their solitude, a solitude tainted with coercion and remorse. The solitude that attracts and fascinates them is the one capable of arousing in them a love both real and bruised, a desire to bloom, an impulse, a soaring flight toward another. But we, Malka, why are we running? And toward what love and what kind of solitude?"

It is cold and I am shivering, yet I am thinking not of the cold but of the night and what it conceals. I am no longer thinking of Katriel but of the woman who links us and also threatens that link. The war is over and I am alive, ready for peace and love. Every limb of my numbed body is ready to make peace and to love gently, without losing itself in hasty, useless gestures. All this should amuse me, yet it no longer does. Gone my need to laugh. Were I to plunge into the flame, would it protect me from the noises

of the earth, from the shadows over there, behind my back?
I want to get up, to gaze at the sky and then set it afire,
once and for all. Gone the shivering from my body. I am
burning.

"Malka," I say. "I want to dance with you. I want to
change the order of the night and its disorder as well. Come,
Malka. Let's dance to the light of the stars, and we'll make
them dance too."

"Yes, yes," she says, "we'll dance up to the stars, there
we shall be safe and you'll no longer resist me, perhaps there
you'll stop running."

My hands are on her waist and the mountains bow to us.
The moon hides slyly behind a fleecy cloud. Do the worshippers notice the moon? Are they watching us? No matter. True, it is a strange hour to be dancing—and a strange
place. But we cannot help it, can we, Malka? An irresistible
force has seized our bodies and sweeps us away in a whirlwind along with the stones and the steps, the stars and the
trees. The sky above the city, the city itself, and the people
dreaming within its gates, all are spinning around us, with
us. Our rhythm is their rhythm, faster, faster; it is increasing
with every passing moment. We dance and bite our lips.
Malka closes her eyes, I keep mine wide open. I want to see
and see again the night and the stars and the mountains and
the walls above and below. They fill me with that tenderness mixed with sadness reserved for what one loves and
knows one soon must lose.

All of a sudden I realize that the sky is filled not with
stars but with funeral candles. I cry out: "Don't look,
Malka, don't look at the stars, they are the eyes of death,
the eyes of the dead stolen by death from the living, the
eyes of Katriel perhaps."

She presses her face against my shoulder, looks up quickly

and replies: "I cannot see the sky, your eyes are all I see."
I look at her and I am aghast. Malka's eyes are not my
mother's eyes, after all; they are the eyes of Ileana, the
woman who by sacrificing her own life had saved mine.

The memory of Ileana brings me back to earth. My wings
are broken, I no longer want to dance with Malka or be
alone with her. It is Ileana I am holding in my arms, it is
her body I am shielding. What has she come to seek here?

Out of breath, we return to our tree stump among the
madmen and beggars, who welcome us with guffaws and
half-serious reproaches. Who cares what they are thinking?
Ileana is beyond their reach. She belongs to my other
memories, forbidden and isolated. The last survivor begs
you not to trespass.

Yet Malka is right. We must confront the present. Come
back to the living.

A sentry approaches, brandishes his flashlight, recognizes
us and goes off to complete his rounds. He says nothing, so
much the better. I could have done without his indulgent
smile. From the Wall the wind blows us bits of prayer, like
a consolation.

"The worst thing," I say to the young woman, who, still
gasping, refuses to release my moist hand, "the worst thing
is to have dead eyes and still be alive."

"You want to bet?" Velvel suggests.

"You starting that again?" Zadok reprimands him.

"Mind your own business," says Velvel.

"It's astonishing just the same," says my blind friend.

"What's astonishing, Shlomo?"

"That you should know what I know."

"I demand an explanation," implores the young pilot.
"What's he talking about? What are you both talking
about?"

"Go ahead," Shlomo says. "We have the right to know."

"I once knew a woman," I say. "I loved her and I saw her die."

"A woman?" Velvel shouts with excitement. "Was she young? Like Malka? Beautiful? Was she Jewish at least?"

"She was older than I. And she was not Jewish."

Velvel feels cheated. He groans in disappointment. Yet he is wrong to disapprove. My love for Ileana was something other than love. I had come back from too far, I had sustained too many wounds to see in her a woman like other women. No, she was not Jewish; her eyes were. And they had followed me here. They will inspire a story in which Katriel has no place. Malka knows this; she covers her mouth, and her teeth chatter with cold.

XII

I T ' S nothing, Ileana thought, nothing but the wind beating against the shutters, trying to enter, and since it can't, it takes revenge by disturbing my sleep.

Light knocks and muffled scratching. Like mice chasing across glass. Ileana opened her eyes and held her breath. Her suspicion gave way to certainty: someone was rapping at the window. The police? They would have smashed the door open by now. An emissary, a liaison officer? Sent by whom? Well, she would go and find out.

Quietly, so as not to awaken the sleeper, she slid from the bed, went over to the curtains and thought she heard the breathing of something as vast as the sea. Moving with caution, she parted the shutters slightly and drew back. In front of her house stood a veritable human tide. And the scratching continued without interruption.

Ileana thought of warning the sleeper. Then she decided against it: why frighten him? The people outside were unaware of his presence. What could they possibly want? Well, she would go out and see for herself. And whatever happened, she would manage alone.

She widened the slit. Those outside caught sight of her, and the din immediately ceased. Several men in front began to gesticulate, inviting her outside. She nodded with disdain.

She took a moment to slip into her dressing gown, then

groped her way to the door, opened it and locked it carefully behind her. When the crowd saw her, a wave of excitement went through its ranks. The young woman of the château was astonishingly beautiful: tense with anger, cold, fierce, ready to lash out and punish. A broad-shouldered man stepped forward.

Ileana raised her hand: "Stop! Who are you?"

Abashed by her harsh, commanding voice, the man froze. Nailed to the ground, his limbs obeyed not him but the woman who used speech like a whip.

"Don't you recognize me? I'm Anton. The overseer."

"What do you want?"

"We have a certain matter to discuss with you."

"At this hour? You must be crazy."

"It's urgent."

"For whom?"

"For us . . . For you."

"Can't it wait until tomorrow?"

"No. It's very urgent."

"What is it about?"

"I told you. A matter of utmost importance. You'll see, you'll agree. Something that concerns all of us. And it can't wait."

"All right. Come closer."

She knew Anton. A brawler and a brute, lascivious, bragging and sneaky. He had worked for her family many years ago, before the war.

"Speak," said Ileana.

"I've come as a friend."

"I don't doubt it. Nobody but a friend would dare disturb me so late at night. I see you've brought the whole village along. I didn't realize I had so many friends."

"We only want your good."

"Thank you. Now I'm waiting for an explanation. It had better be clear and convincing and, above all, brief."

Anton fiddled with an invisible handkerchief and cleared his throat: "We're only concerned with your guest, the one living in your house. We know all about him."

"I invite whom I please. You're not jealous by any chance, are you?"

Anton swallowed with difficulty: "You are wrong to take it so lightly. This is serious. I've already told you we know all about him."

For the first time Ileana sensed that this was going to be a hard struggle. She did not like the overseer's tone. Intuitively she identified him as the enemy, the leader. Well, she would take care of him. He would not last long. She would defeat him. For an instant she wondered if she should try to alert the sleeper. No: this business was between the villagers and herself. Still, she was glad she had had the presence of mind to lock the door.

"Very well," she said, her beauty heightened by the awareness of danger. "We'll go into the barn. You're not satisfied? Too bad. I receive my visitors where I please. For you it will be the barn. Not the living room."

"We'll follow you," said the overseer grimly.

Without turning her head, Ileana crossed the garden. Behind her, she heard the people dragging their feet and cursing as they stumbled over pebbles and fallen branches. Anton grumbled: "What a woman! This won't be easy. No, not easy at all!"

"What time is it?" Ileana asked.

"Two o'clock."

"Make it quick, I for one intend to get some sleep."

"So do we, Ileana, so do we."

She stopped at the entrance to a structure smelling of hay and manure.

"A match," said Ileana. "And wait until I light the lamp."

Anton complied. This is going to be tough, he thought. It won't be easy to break her. What a woman! He spat on the floor. A thousand horsemen wouldn't scare her! Yes, what a woman!

Ileana found her way inside the barn's familiar darkness. She struck the match without trembling. The oil lamp, suspended from the wooden ceiling in a maze of cobwebs, gave off a dirty yellow light.

"Come in and close the door," Ileana ordered.

Surly and blinking in the sudden light, the villagers crowded into the barn, leaving an empty space between themselves and their hostess, who, standing under the lamp, was eying them coldly. Anton took out a cigarette and was reprimanded on the spot.

"I don't permit smoking here," Ileana said.

The overseer obeyed, with a helpless shrug in the direction of the assembly, as if to say: Judge for yourselves, we're dealing with a tigress, not with a woman. Ileana suppressed a smile and thought: No need to worry if I can keep things going like this.

In full command of her movements and reactions, she studied the people facing her. She knew them all. Men with tanned, sun-beaten faces, suspicious women with pointed, hard chins. Heads of families, young men needing to get married, laborers in faded overalls, unpleasant, vindictive-looking stableboys.

"Good evening," she said. "Thank you for dropping in." She raised her voice. "To what do I owe the pleasure of your visit? Speak up!"

Like a schoolboy called to the blackboard, the overseer stepped forward. "I told you . . . It concerns . . . your guest."

"What about him?"

"He's a Jew."

"So what?" she snapped. "That's his business, maybe mine too, but certainly not yours."

"You're wrong. He's a Jew, and therefore this concerns us all. He's endangering you. And us."

"You risk nothing."

"You mean, less than you. That's true. But when it comes to reprisals, one knows where they begin, never where they end."

It's nothing, Ileana thought. I'll find a way out. They have discovered my secret and want to make use of it. Blackmail. They'll ask for money. All right, I'll pay. The Jew will be saved.

"I'm assuming full responsibility," she retorted.

"That's easy to say. Only, the Germans won't agree."

Ileana felt the color drain from her face. But under the yellow light nobody noticed. The Germans! Ileana thought. They know about the Jew. So it isn't a case of blackmail. It's more serious. I must think of another way. Quickly. Her head was spinning with countless ideas, all wild and disorganized.

"Very well," she declared. "You are entitled to an explanation. Yes, there is a Jew staying in my house. Do you know who he is? No, of course not. I myself don't know. A person of his standing cannot afford to disclose his identity."

"That has nothing to do . . ."

"Yes, Anton, it does. It has a lot to do with it. Haven't you noticed peculiar things happening around here lately? Things were quiet before. Now soldiers are ambushed, trains derailed, military installations blown up. All these operations bear one signature. That of the underground. And the visitor—my guest, and I consider it a high privilege to have him as guest—is one of its leaders."

It was not true. The Jew was too young and too weak to belong to any underground—even a Jewish one. She had found him in the forest, covered with blood, half dead. She had taken him home and nursed him, asking no questions.

"You're nothing but a bunch of imbeciles, vulgar and beastly at that," she continued, her anger rising. "You still don't understand? He came to me on orders from the underground, and it was on its orders that I took him in and gave him shelter! How dare you work against the movement which represents our national pride? How dare you ask me questions about someone you'll celebrate tomorrow as hero and leader of our people? Your foolishness is making you wicked, good, but I find your cowardice disgusting . . ."

She harangued her audience with fire and passion, appealing to reason, to patriotism. And while she described the goals and methods of the clandestine but prestigious movement, she clapped her hands, stamped her feet, brandished her fists, her magnificent eyes flashing darkly.

"It's for you we're fighting, for you we're doing the impossible! To set you free, give you back your dignity as citizens! And now, instead of helping, you spy on us! It's ugly and contemptible! I am ashamed!"

They listened, not daring to interrupt. Even the overseer seemed to absorb her words as if they were sacred. Ileana went on to describe the difficult life led by her friends, the anonymous fighters.

"Far from their homes," she insisted, "they sacrifice their nights and sometimes their lives to make you a gift you

153

don't deserve. They too have parents, brothers, lovers. They too would like to drink fresh water and fall asleep in a woman's embrace. Only, before indulging in their pleasures, before enjoying their personal happiness, they fight to defend your honor."

As she spoke, her voice became gentle, friendly, deeply moving, and everybody listened in respectful silence: it was as if she were narrating an ancient heroic epic. Here and there someone voiced approval and admiration: "Yes, yes, it's beautiful, you've got to admit it, those fellows have courage, bravo, hats off, bravo!"

"So there," Ileana concluded. "Now you know everything. I've told you all I know, or, at least, all you're entitled to know. So please go home and let the underground do its work."

No one moved. I've won this round, Ileana thought, but tomorrow I'll have to find him a new hiding place. With these greedy imbeciles, the only question is who'll be the first at the police station.

"Go home," she repeated. "And be careful. Not a word about this meeting. Let it be our secret, our bond. I thank you for that. Goodnight."

Not a single person left. A patch of very dense blue could be seen through the skylight. Morning would soon be here. If only he doesn't wake up, if only he doesn't start looking for me, Ileana thought. She felt overcome by fatigue. The yellow light cast a weird pallor over the faces. Why weren't they leaving?

"What else are you waiting for?" she asked. "Go away now, it's late. I've told you all you need to know."

Anton looked up, on the alert. Her voice had betrayed her. The young woman was sad and therefore vulnerable.

It's now or never, he thought, bracing himself. He launched his attack: "We want your friend."

Ileana faltered but stood straight.

"We have no choice," Anton went on, feigning regret. "The police are fully informed. They've given us twenty-four hours. They want him dead or alive. Put yourself in our place."

This was the turning point. Aggressive by nature, Ileana was ill-at-ease on the defensive. Vileness to her was to be fought only with contempt. Looking at Anton and his supporters, she had the sensation of sinking into a dirty yellowish pond. She was tossing on its surface, the ugly mob still pursuing her, when she saw her friend on the shore. The Jew was shouting to her, but his words were lost in the fog.

"A cigarette," she said.

Anton took two cigarettes out of his pocket. Having won, he lit his own first.

"A light," said Ileana.

Anton gave her a light. This was the most exciting hour of his life.

"I'd like very much to help you," he said condescendingly. "But I'm afraid it's not going to be possible. You know what policemen are like. One doesn't fool around with those fellows. At least not in wartime. I'm sure you understand."

The more he talked, the more confident and superior he became. He soon permitted himself to address her familiarly as "my dear Ileana," then "my little Ileana," and finally, "my poor Ileana."

"If what you say is true—and we respect you too much to doubt your word—if your guest is not your friend, you must turn him over to us. Your scruples may be honorable, but don't let them affect your judgment. Remember, Ileana, that your obligations to your village far outweigh any you may feel to a stranger, and a Jew at that. Would you like to see our homes burned to the ground because of him, because of you, my little Ileana? I am sure you wouldn't think of it, would you?"

Ileana now regretted having locked the door. The sleeper must be warned. By making a noise. By knocking the lamp over. By provoking an uproar, a fire. But Anton was watching her closely, much too closely. She would have to distract him to gain time.

"And you think the underground won't hear about this?" she replied, mastering her dismay. "You think we'll just let it pass and forget the whole incident? Have you thought for a moment of the possible consequences?"

"Don't be angry," Anton said, affecting kindness. "Suppose the underground had to choose between a Jewish refugee and a Christian village. What do you think its choice would be?"

"He's not a Jewish refugee! He's a fighter! A leader! There's a price on his head! The Germans are looking for him, so are their Polish collaborators! His exploits are legendary! He inspires fear and respect even among his adversaries! Do you have any idea what betraying such a man will cost you?"

A sly look in his squinty eyes, Anton was blowing rings of white smoke around the oil lamp. The angrier Ileana became, the more she would be at his mercy. The taste of victory was already in his mouth.

"By the way," he remarked in an offhand way, "what underground movement are you referring to?"

"The Unified Movement, of course! There is no other in our region! You should know that!"

"I'm asking because I greatly admire the way you've been praising its work. You were moving, really. And sincere, so sincere. Yet there is one thing I don't quite understand . . ." He puffed on his cigarette before delivering the final blow. "I don't understand how you can describe underground activity so beautifully, so convincingly, when you've never —never—been part of it. It happens, my poor Ileana, that at this very moment, there stands humbly before you the regional commander of the underground. Now . . ."

Livid with humiliation, Ileana bit her lips. One word, just one, was ravaging her chest and throat, fighting its way out, growing to monstrous proportions, demanding to be spoken.

"Swine!" she hissed.

She wanted to vomit.

"Swine!" she repeated.

The overseer nodded politely, as though he had received a compliment. Ileana turned away and plunged into the crowd. The people respectfully stood aside. She stopped before an old man named Mikolaichik.

"You know me, you knew my father. Haven't you anything to say?" she asked.

"I'm an old man, Ileana. For me each day is a gift."

"What price do you pay for it?"

"At my age one doesn't look at prices any more."

"That's all you have to say, Mikolaichik?"

"At my age, Ileana, there's not much left to say."

"Think! Think carefully! A man's life depends on it! I might even add that it's the life of an innocent man, wrongly persecuted, but that is irrelevant. If you remain silent, you are sentencing him to certain death. If you speak up, he might live. What do you say?"

"At my age, Ileana, one no longer plays at being a judge."

Uncomfortably shifting his feet under her accusing eyes,

Mikolaichik stood his ground, but whimpered: "What do you want from me? Why pick on me? What did I ever do to you? Who am I anyway? Neither judge nor assassin. These are not my decisions, this was not my idea. You wouldn't want me to fight a whole village full of friends and relatives, would you? And then, this Jew, what's he to you? Do you love him? No. Do you owe him something? No. He's a foreigner, a fugitive: forget him! Forget him, Ileana! For your own good, for ours as well, forget him! I beg you, Ileana! It's your duty to us, to the village, to your parents who built it and sustained it . . ."

All Ileana could do was stare at him, so intently, with such pain, that in the end his image dissolved. Instead she saw another: her own, as a young girl. She felt for that child a nameless and impersonal pity. She was playing the piano, and the Jew who was her teacher was saying: "Take it easy, slowly, watch that rhythm, don't rush it, don't rush." — "Do you love him?" No, she didn't love him. It was something else. Did he love her? No, he did not. He was too young, too hurt to love. Their bodies had never touched, but she felt loved in his presence. Also pure and generous. Sometimes, watching over his restless sleep, she could not hold back her tears. She who had never wept as a child. He had guessed that. From the first days, when he was still confined to bed, he would murmur haltingly: "Don't worry. Everything will be fine. I won't die. I cannot die." And another time, later: "Is it because of me that tears come more easily to you than before? I think I have taught you how to cry. For nothing? No. Not for nothing. One never cries for nothing."

"Forget him," Mikolaichik was insisting. "At your age and at mine too, one forgets quickly."

Forget him? Ileana thought. That would be easy. She

knew nothing of his past, none of his secrets. She didn't even know his name. Too discreet to ask. One day he had said to her with a disquieting smile: "I know you're curious. Unfortunately, I'm afraid to speak. Believe me. It would be unwise and dangerous for me to confide in you, more dangerous for you than for me."

Something inside her was telling her: Go, stretch yourself out on the ground, tell them to trample you and spit on you. That's all they want. They've nothing against him, it's you they hate, it's your pride they want to break and debase. Go, tell them you'll submit, you'll accept their revenge. The voice became imperious, but Ileana was not ready to bow. Not yet.

There were other Mikolaichiks in the crowd. They followed her every gesture, every turn of her body. Her head threatened to split, nausea was overcoming her, and yet she kept moving from one person to the next, a dark force pulling her downwards, into the bowels of the earth where eyes and voices die as do memories and passions. Her body, accustomed to pride, did not want to yield. Not yet.

She made the rounds of the people she had known since her eyes first opened on the world. She approached some with a request, others with a compliment, still others with a threat. All rejected her.

Through the skylight the blue was losing its density and becoming translucent. The beginning of a newly born day. Ileana remembered the nights spent at her patient's bedside. "Look," he would say to her. "This is the purest moment. Most people are still asleep when it unfolds; hence its purity and power." Later, while convalescing, he would awaken her and draw her to the window. She had never known such a feeling of peace before.

"Your Jew seems to mean a lot to you," Anton said in a

low voice. "You'd pay anything to save him, right? I have an idea. Give yourself to me, and in exchange—"

"Swine," she threw at him.

"—and in exchange I promise to see what I can do." He sneered obscenely: "Well, how about it?"

Not expecting an answer, he dropped his cigarette and crushed it with his heel, wiping his lips as after a tasty meal or a glass of strong wine. Then he stared at the young woman, seeing her in a new light: his eyes were undressing her, exploring and fondling her tense body. Without diverting his attention from Ileana, he addressed the villagers:

"As your leader, it's my duty to inform you that our young hostess has just made me a rather interesting proposition," he said, scratching his head in pretended embarrassment.

I'm going to collapse, Ileana thought. I should not have locked that door. I should have guessed all this, foreseen it. Now it's too late, too late.

She was dizzy, her heart was pounding furiously. And that dirty yellow light. And that huge cold hand clutching at her throat. Squeezing, tightening. A general uproar followed Anton's declaration. Sneers, insults, curses. The women were doubled over with laughter. Anton, to please them, struck a coquettish pose: he stood before an invisible mirror, combing his hair, fixing his belt and buttoning his shirt.

"Now that's a proposition which ought to.compensate us," the overseer explained. "It's up to you to decide. As for me, I'd be inclined to accept. My wife might hold it against me—and break my neck for it—but what wouldn't I do to save a Jew?"

Several younger Mikolaichiks snickered and poked him in the ribs: "Come, poor Anton, complain, why don't you?"

"You want us to take your place?"

"Help you perhaps?"

"Actually," the overseer continued, "I oughtn't to think just about my own pleasure. I'm not selfish. Let others take advantage of the offer too. We might ask our magnificent and beautiful benefactress to show some charity, no?"

Finally the young woman's body pivoted, sagged and sank slowly to the ground. She lost consciousness. A pharmacist in the crowd revived her. The others encouraged him to examine her more closely:

"Don't be afraid!" they shouted.

"Open her gown!"

"Let's have a look at what she's got to sell!"

Opening her eyes, Ileana saw the overseer bent over her. He was asking insistently: "Where is the key?"

The young woman did not know her eyes were not the same as before; now they reflected emptiness.

"The door is locked," Anton said. "Your beloved Jew may be armed. Be nice, be a good girl. Give me the key. We want to enter your house as friends."

Ileana's mind cleared. "Help me get up," she ordered the overseer. The key, she thought. They don't have it. That means I didn't have it on me. I must have lost it after I closed the door. It must have fallen out of my pocket.

Getting on her feet, she saw one more chance. I'll go with them, pick up the key, open the door. I'll find a way to warn him, to save him.

"I'll go with you," she said.

"You're getting smart. Bravo!"

The key. The house. The door. I'll yell, Ileana thought. But her plan failed. Her voice betrayed her at the very moment she needed it most.

In the darkness, the room seemed peaceful and serene.

Nothing stirred. Ileana stood framed in the doorway, looking over the men's backs. Spent and numb, she acknowledged defeat.

What followed had the precision of a prearranged nightmare. Gliding stealthily, like ghosts caught in a ghoulish ballet, Anton and three of his aides surrounded the bed. Under the crumpled bedclothes, the crouching body seemed to be expecting them. In one sweeping movement, following the choreography of some ancient occult ritual, they raised their arms high in the air and lowered them slowly, very slowly, until, at a signal from the overseer, they plunged their daggers into their victim.

The leader's roar came suddenly: "He's gone! He has escaped!"

Dazed, the young woman nearly fainted again. She noticed the open window. So did Anton. Several men rushed outside to catch the fugitive; they returned empty-handed.

"Where is he?" Anton shouted. "Tell us! Tell us where he went!"

"I don't know, I don't know anything," she answered in a faltering voice.

"You'll pay for this! I'll make you pay for this . . ."

Ileana looked at him without seeing him, without even understanding what he wanted from her. She went over to stretch out on the bed and seemed surprised to find it empty. Her eyes were burning, and she thought: They are not mine.

Only when she saw the daggers' reflection in the cold black eyes surrounding her did she realize the miracle was not imagined: her friend's life was safe. It was then her body relented and allowed her voice a scream of liberation. It proclaimed joy and sacrifice. And it invited madness.

XIII

A N D the game went on, it still does.
The survivor has surmounted trials and punishments. Houses
in flames, roads blown to pieces no longer concerned him.
More than once the world had crumbled around him and
yet he would rise unharmed, as after a rehearsal. He couldn't
tell why he was saved and not this friend or that mentor.
He still can't. If indeed this was a game, he is acquainted
neither with its rules nor with his opponent.

Yet, thanks to Katriel, I thought I could draw the final
line. I had actually convinced myself. This war in the making would certainly break my chains and bring the contest
to its ultimate conclusion.

I see myself with Katriel again, at the time of our last
meeting. He is telling me about his childhood, and I com-
pare it with mine. He speaks to me of his plans and I am
silent; I have none. He says "Tomorrow," and I know that
tomorrow I shall die.

Why tomorrow and why in this land? Because I am forty
and Jewish? Because the survivor is tired of running after
the dead? No matter. You want tomorrow, let it be tomorrow, may Your will be done, at least this time, amen.

I try to imagine the event: where will I be? Buried beneath the rubble of which fortification? Abandoned in

which desert? I torture my fantasy, I spur it on, but it rebels: impossible to make it obey. If the future exists, my imagination refuses to place me in it. Will I be disfigured by tank treads? Try as I may, I cannot see myself as a corpse. Well, patience. Besides, who said I would fall in battle? Or that war would erupt tomorrow? The circumstances are unimportant. During maneuvers perhaps. Why not? A stray bullet. A grenade thrown one second too early or too late. A mine lost or forgotten. Curtain. End.

A mosquito buzzes on my cheek. I crush it. Perhaps it too knew what was in store for it.

Tomorrow, I think, and my calm astonishes me. A slight chill in the shoulders and spine. Orderly, lucid thoughts, forming a shield no past will ever pierce. There is such plenitude in this moment that it seems timeless and perhaps eternal. I have never felt so alive. And so strong is this sensation, so sudden the change, that I need to hear the sound of a voice, my own.

"Katriel . . ."

"Yes?"

"What are you thinking about?"

"War. War transforms all who take part in it. I wonder in what way?"

"Are you afraid?"

"Yes, I'm afraid."

"Will you keep your promise?"

"Of course. You will too."

I say nothing.

"I wonder how you'll go about doing it," he adds. "How will you speak as witness?"

He is expecting an answer, but I don't feel like talking any more. I want to be alone.

"Look at me," I ask.

His brooding gaze is on me.

"Now please go."

Taken by surprise, he lingers, undecided, and shakes his head reproachfully. Then, more hurt than offended, he turns on his heel and disappears into the darkness of the tent.

As for me, I feel overcome with pity. Pity for Katriel, for his fellow men. Pity for the world which will survive me.

I stretch and breathe in the cool air. Night is stirring in the woods beyond the valley. Where could I go now? I take a few steps, and stop to listen, trying to comprehend. Transparent, icy clouds chase one another across a cold and boundless sky. Pale and fleeting, the moon shows markings of blue, gray and yellow. On the other side, the mountains of Judea: close yet impenetrable. In the distance, beyond the orange groves and fragrant palms, the dark city seems poised on its haunches, its fists clenched over a thousand black sparks. With its tents stretching to infinity and its fires extinguished, the camp looks unreal, harboring crouching, voiceless shadows waiting for dawn, to spring back into action, into sight, to fly toward the sun and there proclaim the joy of living, the need for dying. Stop! Who goes there? A king turned shepherd again, a prophet in search of his vision, his voice? Is it possible, then, that the earth remembers man? A shooting star shimmers and falls. Say, watchman, what of the night? Morning will come, and so will war, and so will death. As always. Wars follow and resemble one another; and death follows and resembles them. And all the tears, all the vows of love and friendship will not prevent the blood from flowing or the dawn from bearing its colors. And all the miracles in the world will not prevent suffering and injustice from having existed forever and triumphed so often. The traveler will confirm it to you:

he returned to his village and found his dwelling in ruins. Is that the end of the tale? I don't know. Not yet. I shall know in a few days, a few hours. How many hours, how many days? Say, sentinel, what of the end? Only the Angel of Death knows the answer, and he is hiding behind God, of whom Rabbi Mendel of Kotzk used to say that He is to be found wherever He is permitted to enter. Impossible to separate the two presences, the two calls of eternity. And man? Say, watchman, what of man? The Messiah will come, and so will silence, and so will the end—which is the end of mourning as well. So move aside, save yourself, his breath burns everything along his way. Watchman, open your eyes and be prepared!

I feel anguish gripping me again. Could this really be the end? I peer into the darkness around me, inside me, expecting a sign, an echo. Everything blurs. Images and clues disintegrate. Disguised as a beggar, the preacher is pointing to a blind old man: he is at once Katriel's father, mine and myself. A woman sobs quietly: it's you, Malka, it's Ileana, it's my mother. Then I find myself thrust into a town I recognize without ever having visited it, lost in a hostile crowd yelling: "Catch him, catch him!" I shout . . . A madman seizes me and says: "You're in grave danger, give me your face." I give it to him and wake up, perspiring profusely and in such a state of fury that it takes me a long time to calm down.

Around me, everything appears quiet, deceptively quiet. Hushed whispers over there, near the command post. Noises of cars stopping, starting. A door opens, closes. Somewhere a courier is being interrogated, offered a drink and sent off, relieved or burdened with concern. Are the dice cast, the decisions made? For whom and for when? Could we have gained a day, after all? Who then is trustee of our time, our freedom? Does someone already know what each will have to accomplish at what moment, in what place, in order to defeat the enemy, whoever he may be, in order simply to win and survive, or die?

In the distance, the city is sleeping, or pretending to. Katriel is resting, or pretending to. How will he behave as witness? How will he tell the tale? He'll find a way. He'll say: I saw my friend before he died, he was pretending to prepare for his departure.

Katriel will speak, he will not forget our pact. Bravo, Katriel. Thank you, Katriel. I try to evoke his face: it hides from me. Too bad. I'll invent it, I'll draw it again, starting from scratch. So, player, how long will the game go on? Watchman, what of the game? Watchman, what of life? It is too late to live, too late to love. May the devil take you, watchman, and the night! I'm not playing any more, I quit the play. May memory take you, watchman! It's too late to remember, too late to keep watch.

A picture: another night, another place. Gathered in a courtyard, under a blue sky flecked with blood, anxious neighbors are awaiting the return of my father gone to make inquiries. After an hour or two he appears. His features are drawn, his eyes are troubled. I had never seen him look so helpless. Assailed by questions, he could only repeat the same words over and over: "It's for tomorrow, it's for tomorrow."

And without realizing it, as I free myself from the mysterious city where time no longer counts, saved from oblivion but not from death, I too begin to murmur: "It's for tomorrow, it's for tomorrow."

XIV

AND the war began, not the following dawn, but three hours later. And like all of you, my nocturnal companions, I lived through it in a trance, battered by one surprise after another, going through horror only to end up in euphoria. As long as I remained alive, I had to see everything, retain everything. And I, who blur the centuries, suddenly found myself capable of grasping certain events as they unfolded, hour by hour, particularly in the beginning, during the first phase of the operation. I was caught in the machinery.

I remember: we were devouring our breakfast amid the usual hubbub when suddenly we heard the rumbling of jets taking off from the nearby air base. No one seemed troubled by it, not even curious. We thought: Those pilots are lucky, at least they're doing something useful. Their reconnaissance and surveillance missions are more exciting than infantry drills.

After the meal I went over to Gad's headquarters. He had one hand on the field phone and did not return my greeting. Bent over his maps, he was not studying them; he seemed far away. A strange smile of relief and resignation hovered in his blue eyes, which seemed to be parting regretfully with an abstract and distant dream. It was as though he were permitting himself one more time the luxury of meditating on man's destiny and his own. It made him look younger. I saw before me the adolescent I had known in Europe, happy and unhappy for the same reasons as then. Was it intuition on my part?

"This is it, isn't it?" I said after a pause.

"Yes, this is it."

"Since when?"

"More than an hour ago. On the southern front."

"How does it look?"

"Too soon to tell. No news for the moment. But everything is going well, yes, everything is going well."

Alerted, his staff officers burst in all at once and began reviewing topographical maps and logistical plans, sector by sector, point by point, weighing hypothetical situations and unforeseeable, unimaginable obstacles.

Orders from General Headquarters were clear, precise: Take no initiative, avoid opening a second front. Wait and see. Respond to limited provocations, nothing more, nothing else. But a change of tactics was not excluded. Everything depended on the other side's intentions.

It was not yet known in camp that the apocalypse had already swept into the desert. Sergeants and corporals were inspecting tents, mobile kitchens, irritating the troops by getting irritated over nothing: they were playing at war in the shadow of war, without hearing its explosions, without sensing in any way that for some of us there was not much time left to live, not much time left to play. The sky offered itself, pure and deeply blue, to a fiery, vengeful sun. The treetops swayed, the sounds of the breeze in harmony with those of the earth.

The door of the command post opened to let the officers

hurry out, each running to his unit. A moment later the camp was unrecognizable. An hour later the battalion was ready to move.

From the old walled city, the legionnaires had already begun shelling the Jewish quarter of Jerusalem: a sporadic, confused fire. Was this the prelude to a full-scale offensive? A large concentration of heavy artillery gave the answer. Though poorly aimed, it sowed destruction in the suburbs. Now that the second front had opened, Gad requested the green light for his tanks. It was granted. Staff members who were present admired his restraint:

"So, it's Go?"

"Yes."

"As agreed? According to plan?"

"Yes."

"And the big stake?"

"Not yet."

"But I am telling you we can take it! I have the means!"

A categorical "No" ended the transmission.

Gad concealed his discontent by recapitulating the elements of the situation. The principal effort of the Army Corps was to make a lightning push westward to reach the Jordan. Speed would be the decisive element of the campaign.

"Occupy the cities," Gad said. "Surround all pockets of resistance and proceed with the attack. Leave the mopping up for later. Undertake no action which would risk breaking the initial thrust. Objectives assigned to our battalion: re-establish ground contact with the Mount Scopus enclave, and occupy the heights dominating the Jordanian sector of Jerusalem. H-hour: 22:00. Any questions?"

Yes. One. Only one. A bearded captain, his hand raised, formulated it succinctly: "And the Old City?"

"It'll be encircled and sealed off."

Though there was not the slightest hint of reproach, Gad felt it necessary to explain, to justify himself: "You're disappointed, so am I. There is nothing I can do about it. Orders from High Command, you know. But . . ." He let his gaze wander over his staff with a half-dreamy, half-amused expression, then added: "But don't worry. Before this war is over we shall be in the Old City."

The captain blinked and asked: "Promise?"

"Yes. And when the moment comes, I hope you'll keep my promise to capture it."

It was almost evening—evening comes quickly in the mountainous areas of Jerusalem—when Gad, who stayed in constant communication with Division Headquarters, was informed that the government, encouraged by the victories in the Sinai, had revised its earlier decision: "You asked for the big stake? It's ours, Gad, it's yours."

The news was greeted in camp by roaring applause. The war had suddenly changed character and dimension. We now prepared ourselves with enthusiasm for a rendezvous with history. We did not eat, we did not even write the traditional pre-battle letters to be delivered home, just in case. All companies volunteered for the first attack. Tanks, half-tracks and machine guns had never been in such perfect condition. In the general excitement, friends embraced, strangers shook hands and smiled at one another with pride.

"You'll come with me," Gad said.

"Thanks. But I'd only be in your way. I'll be all right where I am."

"Are you sure?"

"Positive."

"All right then. But don't get yourself killed. Understand?"

For a moment my heart pounded wildly, and the blood rushed to my temples. Standing in my friend's office, both of us in battle dress, I wanted to do something, say something to mark the end of our adventure, our friendship. But we were not alone. Pressed from all sides and surrounded by his aides, Gad was already plotting lines on a map.

"Good luck, Gad."

"Be careful," he answered, eying me fleetingly. "Be very careful."

"Good luck, friend."

With a heavy heart, I returned to my unit, which was receiving its final instructions from Yoav. When asked if I wanted a gun, I answered no, I wouldn't know how to use it.

"Jerusalem," said Katriel. "We are going to Jerusalem. My father will be pleased. Whatever the outcome, he will be pleased."

He seemed less exalted than anxious.

SHORTLY before 21:00 Gad informed DHQ that his troops would move into the field soon. Under cover of night, two squads of Engineering Corps, their tools in hand, were already crawling noiselessly toward the area they were to clear of mines and barbed wire. Under their yellow-green camouflage, the tanks were adjusting their cannons. The paratroopers of the first wave held the forward positions, hugging the ground, becoming one with it and the silence above. My platoon, under the command of Lieutenant Arieh, a daredevil barely past adolescence, was assigned to reinforcements. A three-story house was our shelter. Gad improvised his advanced command post on the roof of the building opposite. In the cellar, the Medical Corps was setting up an emergency station. An old woman walked among us, distributing hot coffee and sandwiches. She refused to be evacuated.

"But, grandmother," Arieh pleaded with her, "this place isn't safe! You should go below, stay in the shelter!"

"I'm not afraid," she answered. "And I'm so grateful that you chose my house. And besides, who will look after you?"

All the gentleness, all the pain of Israel were in her resolute voice. I wanted to see her face but couldn't; it was too dark in the room.

I do remember, however, that she was the most serene of us all.

2 2 : 0 0 .

With a roar powerful enough to herald and provoke the end of the world, the night abruptly burst into flame, setting fire to the horizon beyond the mountains and valleys, turning into a thousand-mouthed monster, spewing heat and horror and death.

We jumped to our feet without waiting for orders. We rushed headlong into the street, where units of the second and third waves were forming. The sergeant quickly called the roll to establish if anyone was missing. Arieh, in radio contact with Gad, motioned Yoav to come closer.

"Are we off, Lieutenant?"

"Soon. As soon as they break through."

The artillery duel was gaining in intensity. To protect the infantry, tanks and recoilless cannons went ahead to pulverize enemy bunkers and batteries. On one side, the shattering din of exploding shells, and silence on the other. Penetration of one by the other. Both kept me under their spell. A thought: men only kill men, they are powerless against silence. I leaned over to Katriel to share my discovery with him: "Do you know what war is? A journey to the end of silence."

Katriel was watching the paths traced by thousands of projectiles in the black night. "It's terrible," he said, "but I can't help finding all this beautiful."

After the artillery, the heavy machine guns went into action. The real attack, human this time, was just beginning. In the savage onslaught, bodies rose, rebounded and fell, disemboweled. In order to reach the enemy trenches, we had to crawl through five rows of barbed wire. Screams of battle, screams of the wounded, orders shouted and repeated endlessly. Every heart was the mutilated heart of the night, every tear a tribute to its cruelty.

Just when did we climb into which vehicle? And when did it rumble off in which direction? When did we leave it? I no longer remember. I recollect only the deafening thunder enveloping my whole being. I was nothing more than a noise, repudiated by the receding silence.

Jostled, buffeted, pushed forward and sideways, I found myself in no man's land, swept along by Sergeant Yoav, who was running and shouting like a madman, stopping only briefly here and there to prod the laggards. He seemed to have more than two eyes, more than two arms. He saw all of his men, and nothing they did—or didn't do—escaped him. He had only one single word on his lips—"Faster, faster!"—but by varying his tone he managed to convey every shade of human feeling. Without transition he went from anger to softness, to supplication. What mattered was to keep moving, to advance as far as possible, as quickly as possible.

And like the others, I was caught in the mechanism. All my plans, all my resolutions to cling to my awareness and take note of everything were left in suspense behind me, outside me. The wounded evacuated to the rear, scouts blown to bits, I passed them all without seeing them. Like the others, I climbed when I had to climb, crawled when I was told to crawl: like the others, I followed the sergeant the way one follows an irascible, omnipotent father who protects his children by leading them to glory, and also to sacrifice. Like the others, I breathed in the night and the smoke, I was drenched in sweat, I shouted anything at anyone, echoing the calls and warnings rising from the battlefield, amplified by terror and darkness:

"Watch out! Mines!"

"A bunker! Away from there!"

"Grenade going off!"

"Don't move! To your right!"

"A sniper!"

"Get him! Get him!"

"Medic! Here! Medic! I've been hit! Hiiittt!"

I was not wounded, not yet, but I shouted with the one who was, and for him:

"Third platoon, over here!"

"Shayke, your flamethrower!"

"Uzi! What are you waiting for! For heaven's sake, let them have it!"

Shells were raining down, yellowish lightning flashes were streaking the night and peopling it with mutilated, disfigured phantoms screaming, moaning, crying their pain and madness, and also with the dying, friend and enemy alike, clamoring for help. They could see nothing, recognize no one. They were all interchangeable yet unique, immortal yet in agony, inhumanly savage yet totally, painfully human.

"Down! Idiot! Down!"

Someone, a stranger, saved my life. For how long? Irrelevant. I wasn't thinking of that any more. I was thinking of nothing. At that moment, in that formless and bloody scramble, there was only one thing to do, and I did it unconsciously: run, run forward without looking, without listening, run in response to any order, any reflex, giving up thoughts which had lost their weight and their hold over me, run to pursue a silence which in turn backed away into darkness to mingle with the living waves, opening and closing with irresistible force, and leaving in their wake a violent and nauseating odor of sulphur and blood.

Fortifications and sniper nests wiped out, casements gutted, machine guns and gunners twisted and charred, vehicles overturned, automatic weapons crackling, deafening mortar explosions overhead, everywhere: this was my baptism by fire, and I went through it like an experienced if reckless warrior.

"Hey, you!" a noncom shouted at me. "Where the hell's your gun?"

"I have none, never had."

"Here, catch!"

At the touch of the rifle, reality exploded in my consciousness with blinding force. I fingered the weapon and found it heavy and cumbersome. To whom had it belonged? I held it away from me, fearful of its whims, and yet I didn't dare dispose of it. I felt useless, ridiculous, superfluous in this war I was fighting by proxy. If I died, it would be said I had fallen in combat, and that would be false. Fortunately, Katriel would be there to establish the facts. But where was he? I shouted: "Katriel, Katriel!" No sign of Katriel. "Yoav, Yoav!" No sign of Yoav. Nor of Arieh. Nor of Gdalia. Cut off from my unit, separated from Katriel. Panic seized me. I laid down the rifle and started to run again. I stumbled over a huge rock, a girder. No: a corpse. A shiver of disgust, of horror: my first corpse. There it lay, before me, huge, shriveled, blood trickling from its mouth. One of ours? How could I know? This was no time to identify corpses. I must keep moving, I thought. Further ahead, a second corpse, arms crossed, barring access to a craggy road. All the corpses of that night had been laid before me, they had all joined in a conspiracy against me. Well, ignore them. Only solution. Don't look, pay no attention. Don't think. Pass by. Jump. Eyes closed. I ran a long time without reopening them. Shlomo, the blind Hasid, that's me: I no longer cared where I was running, whom I was trampling. Then I heard the noise of a motor. A car. There it was, alongside me. Yes, it was Gad.

"Get in," he shouted without slowing down.

Arms were gripping me, hoisting me onto an open half-track. Gasping, I felt close to fainting. I struggled to catch my breath. And to suppress the sob threatening to choke me. Though seated, I felt I was still running, sucked in by the void. And while running I asked Gad: "How is it going?" He didn't answer. Because, in fact, I had not uttered a sound. I tugged at his sleeve; he saw my distorted face and understood.

"Everything is fine, fine, fine."

"Fine, fine," I said, echoing him.

"There are obstacles. Heavy losses. But we're breaking through."

"We're breaking through," I repeated after him. "Breaking through, breaking through."

How long did we speak? How long did we ride? An hour. Maybe less. Infinity was overtaking us. I thought the war, the night, would never end. Quite the opposite, their strength seemed renewed. Once again the horizon seemed on fire. Yet the artillery barrage had ceased. It took me a moment to realize: dawn was breaking. Victorious and aglow, it was reclaiming its gold and its violence from dusk in order to set ablaze the hours, the bushes, the clouds. Was night leaving us? So soon? Thrust out of time, I thought that the attack had just been launched, and also that it had lasted forever and ever and ever. And above all men at war, all creatures steeped in night, pain and victory, there was the voice of Gad: "Arieh, your position!"

"Half a mile from objective."

The young, excited voice of my lieutenant. And where was his platoon? I was hoping Gad would ask him, but he didn't go into details.

"Uzi?"

"Advancing on target three."

"Shlomo?"

"Aviezer here. The captain is wounded."

"Why didn't Motti assume command?"

"Wounded too."

Yonah, Pinhas, Naphtali, Mordecai, Abir: their voices, harsh, exhausted, slow, tense, followed one another, each using the same words, expressing the same confidence.

"How many men do you have left?"

"Enough."

"You need reinforcements?"

"No, thanks. We'll manage."

All along the central front, in rainbow shape, we had already broken through in all sectors. We were moving forward but paying the price. The enemy resisted assaults, fought rear battles with bravery, disregarding danger in a manner not seen in earlier conflicts. Positions were abandoned only after the last defender emptied his last cartridge. Here and there soldiers were locked in close combat, knives between their teeth. Result: out of a company numbering one hundred and twenty, only twelve were still in condition to carry on the offensive. But they were advancing. The radio continued to sputter. A monotonous sputtering, interrupted by unidentifiable battle noises and anonymous agonies. A lieutenant had been killed while reporting to Gad. A sergeant was shouting: "Nadav speaking, Nadav, Fifth Company, we are only six, six of us left, five . . ."

"Your position?" Gad asked.

Nadav kept on repeating: "Five of us left, five, five, only five."

Gad knew most of these men. He found his way with ease through this labyrinth of voices and death rattles. To guess the battle's progress, I was reduced to scrutinizing his face. We were being fired upon, but he remained impassive. I was being fired upon, and oddly enough I saw the sun turning on its axis and fall with dizzying speed; then incredibly I saw it down below, lying on the ground, covered with burning dust, looking like a crushed black crow.

"IT'S nothing," the doctor said. "Just a scratch."

I knew he was wrong.

"And the others?" I asked. "Gad? And the driver? And the radioman?"

"Safe and sound."

Gad had brought me here.

"When?"

"Two hours ago. Maybe three."

I tried to sit up, leaning on my elbows, but had to lie down again. A sharp pain pierced my left arm and shot toward the brain.

"It's nothing," said the doctor. "Just a scratch."

It wasn't true, but he couldn't know that.

"I'd like to leave, rejoin my unit as soon as possible."

"No objection."

He wished to reassure me about my condition, so he told me what had happened: "The bullet just missed you. One of your friends saw it coming and pushed you out of the car. You fell, lost consciousness, and that's how you were saved. You could—and should—undergo a more thorough checkup. Later. Not now. We're swamped."

In the tent, dozens of young men were groaning while waiting to be transferred to hospitals in town.

"Take a little rest," the doctor said. "You'll need all your strength. The war isn't over yet. And . . ."

Summoned to an emergency, he didn't finish his sentence. I got up and went out, unsteady on my legs. An officer, his head bandaged, was getting into his jeep.

"Could you tell me where I might find *Sgan Aluf* Gad?" I asked.

"Get in."

I wanted to question him, about the fate of the Old City, the war in general, but he was in no mood to chat. As he drove, he leaned heavily on the wheel; he must have been in great pain.

We rode in silence for ten minutes or so. Here and there we passed a soot-streaked tank, its treads in midair, like an animal sleeping on its side. Farther down, at the edge of the bumpy road, soldiers were resting under trees left unharmed by the tempest. After another stretch of road, we reached a town teeming with soldiers, and stopped in front of a building less damaged than the others: the battalion's new command post.

Gad was not there, his deputy informed me: he was in conference at Division Headquarters. Would I like to await his return?

"I'd rather catch up with my unit."

"As you like."

Lack of sleep made him appear indifferent.

"Where is it?"

"What?"

"My unit."

"You mean what's left of it? You'd better inquire outside."

I rushed into the street.

A sergeant pointed to a door: "If you're looking for Yoav, he's in there."

Yoav was inside, not Katriel.

"Where are . . . the others?"

He handed me a bottle of soda water: "Drink. In this damned heat you never get enough to drink."

"Yoav, whom did we lose?"

"The lieutenant. Gdalia. Yes, the little Yemenite gambler. And Zvi. The student. You didn't know him. Killed. Amram. Peretz. Bernard Kehati. Evacuated to the rear."

"And . . . Katriel?"

"Oh, he's all right. He's around here somewhere."

I finally found him. Sitting on the sidewalk, facing an abandoned house, he seemed to be sleeping with his eyes open. I sat down beside him but he took no notice. I was the first to speak. In brief and concise terms I told him of my adventures, ending with an account of the strange sensation upon awakening in the emergency station: I was wounded but didn't know exactly where.

"And you?" I asked.

"Me? What about me?"

His voice had changed. It had become harsh, impersonal.

"What happened to you, Katriel?"

For a second he showed me a face so savage and angry I could hardly recognize it. He turned away immediately.

"What do you want to know?" he yelled in a sudden

fit of temper. "You want to know whether I've killed? Is that it?"

He was trembling with rage, with hatred perhaps.

"Yes, I have killed! You want to know whom? And how many times? I don't know myself! I shall never know! And it's of no importance. I've killed and nothing is important any more. Tell me, is that what you wanted to know?"

I couldn't believe my eyes, my ears. I didn't know how to answer. What could possibly appease him? Did he want to be appeased? Perhaps he wished to be judged, condemned. He alone could tell. I was waiting for what was coming next and for the end. Katriel looked at me and began to cry, then to laugh, then to laugh and cry at the same time:

"And you still believe one can know people and what they do! That one can understand and transmit things one feels and fears! Poor, poor David! My friend, ally and witness! Go away! I pity you, and I don't want to pity you! Leave me alone! You consider yourself innocent, and you understand nothing about innocence, and neither do I!"

"Yes, Katriel, I do understand. I understand that you need rest."

"Is that all I need? Is that all you understand?"

I watched him closely. Had the war contaminated him, even him, with its poison, its hatred?

"Leave me alone, please."

I left with a bitter taste in my mouth.

"SO you're all right," Gad said when I entered his new office later that afternoon.

"Just a scratch."

"You're lucky. You got off easy."

"Thanks to my protectors."

"You'll be careful next time. Promise? I won't always be around to throw you out of cars."

"Yes, sir. At your service, sir."

Though his features were gaunt with tension and fatigue, he seemed calm, alert, in full control. Before dismissing me, he brought me up to date on the latest developments: we were going from victory to victory, outdoing ourselves; the enemy forces in Sinai had been routed; the whole nation had kept its promise.

"And the Old City?"

"The big stake? We'll take it tomorrow. Morning."

We shook hands, and I returned to my lodgings. Yoav showed me where to sleep: "The floor is a bit hard, but you won't notice."

I stayed awake awhile, looking out the window. The curfew had transformed the place into a ghost town. Yesterday, only yesterday, a man I shall never know stood in this very spot. What thoughts had gone through his mind?

"Go to bed," Yoav said. "The night will pass quickly. And then . . ."

The people of this village, where were they? Where were the children who had lived in this house yesterday, only yesterday?

"Don't you hear well?" said Yoav, irritated.

I stretched out on the floor. Frustrated. I would have preferred going out for a walk. Forbidden. Dangerous. Not all caves had been cleaned out, not all civilians had been screened. Cases of sabotage had already been reported. Result: strict curfew. Well, let's try to sleep. But I couldn't close my eyes. The more I tried, the more sleep eluded me. Once more I fell prey to fever and irrational anguish. I had reached the limits of fatigue, of consciousness. Tomorrow had lost its meaning.

"So we'll soon be in Jerusalem," said a voice, Katriel's voice.

He sounded like himself again. Good for him, for me too. Hastily I gathered my memories of the night before and our voices of long ago. I won't hold today's outburst against you, Katriel. We must find our dreams again. Now. Jerusalem so near, and yet so far. Alive, accessible. I caught myself speaking to the child I once was. Make me laugh. Just once. Laugh as I've never laughed before. I want to laugh for yesterday, for tomorrow. For Katriel, who was wrong to give in even if only briefly; laugh too for Gad, who resisted too well. I want to laugh and it is my laughter I wish to offer to Jerusalem, my laughter and not my tears.

I see myself back in my town, back in my childhood. Yom Kippur. Day of fasting, of atonement. That evening one cry bursts with the same force from every heart: "Next year in Jerusalem." On my right, among the men draped in their prayer shawls, there was one who did not pray. The next morning I saw him again at the entrance of the Bet Hamidrash, among the beggars and simple-minded. I offered him some change; he refused. "I do not need it, my child," he said. I asked him how he subsisted. "On dreams," he answered.

During Sukkot, the Feast of Tabernacles, I discovered him again in the Borsher Rebbe's wooden hut among the Hasidim singing at the top of their voices.

"Let's go outside," said the beggar. "I'll make you a gift of my dreams." We sat down under a poplar. "I dreamed I was walking on the road. In the distance I saw the Temple burning. I began to run, but the ground beneath kept pulling me back. The Temple was going up in flames, and yet I did nothing to save it." — "I don't like that dream," I said. — "Neither do I. Let's try to change it, shall we? Let me start

again: I dreamed I was walking on the road. In the distance
I saw the Temple more resplendent than ever. I began to
fly toward it. A moment later I had lost my legs. Result:
I had to go on flying, to go on dreaming." — "I don't like
that dream either." — "That's your right, my child. Let's
start again: I dreamed I was walking on the road. In the
distance I saw the Temple ablaze. To save it I had to sing.
But I had lost my tongue. I looked for it in vain in the sand
and in the clouds; it was not there. In desperation I un-
earthed the bodies, shook the ones still alive, examined every
jaw: my tongue was nowhere to be found. I'm looking for
it still, and as long as my breath holds out, I shall continue
to look. Sometimes I glimpse it in the mouth of another,
and then I howl in his face: 'Don't try so hard to fool me,
you won't succeed; don't use my tongue to praise man's
strength and his right to consolation.' I am not often heeded,
it doesn't matter. It's enough for me to know. The Temple
is burning and joy is dead; and if it were not dead, the
orphan that I am would kill it with his own hands." I didn't
like that dream either, I didn't like any of his dreams. Refusing to listen, I attempted to escape, but the beggar held
me back by force. Wryly, he went on, his voice growing
more insistent: "Since you don't appreciate my dreams, I'll
tell you about my life. One morning, in my sleep, I dreamed
that I was sleeping, that I was dreaming that I had awakened.
You will ask: Is that all? Yes, child. That's all. That's already too much." Free from his grasp at last, I was about
to flee. His voice pursued me: "Know, child, that the day
your life will be told to you . . ."

I fell sick and would not sleep. I was afraid to close my
eyes, afraid to discover myself in another dream of yet another beggar. Grandmother rushed to the rabbi and brought
me back his blessing. Mother called the doctor, who spoke

of fatigue, anemia; he gave me an injection, wrote out several prescriptions. "You must rest and calm yourself," he said. "You'll feel better. Tomorrow. You'll see. You'll be a new person. Close your eyes and sleep." I protested: "I don't want to sleep, I don't want to dream, I don't want tomorrow to come." Even after I fell asleep, my moaning continued to spread anxiety throughout the household.

"You're shaking," said Katriel. "So am I. It's because of Jerusalem, isn't it? One doesn't go to Jerusalem, one returns to it. That's one of its mysteries."

And without alluding to his earlier breakdown, he began to reminisce. Twenty years ago he had taken part in the siege of the Old City. He was inside, with the last company defending the last positions. The situation was going from bad to worse. They lacked men and ammunition. Cut off from the Jewish sector, they couldn't even hope to get reinforcements. Yet they were fighting for every ruin, every brick. One evening, out of nowhere, there appeared among the exhausted fighters a queer sort of man who offered them his assistance. The commanding officer couldn't help laughing. "So, you're our reinforcements?" His kaftan in tatters, his face gaunt and solemn: what could he be but a *mekubal*, a mystical madman and visionary, one of those crazy creatures who haunted the Old City for centuries. Offended, the visitor commented: "You're wrong to reject me." — "But how can you be of assistance, grandfather?" — "I could stay with you." — "That's all?" — "That's enough." — "All right," the commander decided. "It's better than nothing." The old man thanked him, and every evening, at dusk, he appeared —no one knew from where—and kept them company until morning. Oddly, the men grew fond of him. Not wanting to lose him, they resisted with more tenacity, more efficiently. He would arrive, carrying a jug of water, a crust of bread. No one could discover where he was hiding himself and his supplies. What was his name? His age? He scoffed at questions: "I don't like curiosity, only passion attracts me." Because of him, the defenders did not sink into apathy. He raised their morale by stirring their imagination. Each one saw him differently. He was the Prophet Elijah comforting the forsaken and the wounded, he was King David bursting with vigor, he was the poet Yehuda Halevi slain at the foot of the Western Wall.

"And then?" I asked.

"Then what?"

"What finally happened to him?"

"Nothing. Shortly before the end he offered us his services as a scout. He claimed he could save us. He said: 'I know this area better than you, better than anyone, I've been living and hiding here a long time. Let me help you. I will show you an underground network of tunnels and you'll be able to hit the enemy from the rear. You'll take him by surprise. Agree and I'll guide you to victory; agree and I'll entrust you with the keys to an invisible city which no power has ever violated.' But the commanding officer, weary and disillusioned, answered him: 'We thank you, friend. Too bad you've come so late, too late. In order to fight, we need men, weapons and ammunition; stories won't do, they are not enough.' He was right. All we had left were ten bullets for each gun. His body stooped, reflecting his sorrow, the old man left. The next day we laid down our arms."

"And the beggar?" I asked.

"How do you know he was a beggar?"

"Just a thought."

"I never saw him again. He was undoubtedly evacuated with the civilians." And after a pause: "No, I don't believe it. I'd rather believe that he remained behind. In the Old City. He's still there. Hiding in the confines of his invisible kingdom. I even believe that he could have saved it from occupation. He could have spared us the capitulation. We were wrong to reject his offer, to depend on our strength rather than his. But the commander belonged to the new generation which boastfully installed a reign of physical courage and ethical pragmatism. In the eyes of that generation, a people can and must alter its destiny. It believes that the children of Israel can escape the past of Israel. Thus it wishes them all to be healthy, normal, cured of obsessions and complexes, relieved of mystery and burden. It is deluding itself. And this war proves it. We have known and experienced threats and perils more than once. Nothing is new, nothing has changed. Scenario, plots, scenery, characters: the curtain needed only to be raised. As in the past, what was wanted was our death. As in the past, solitude is our mark of distinction. The beggar knew it. That was why he offered us his own methods, his own weapons: they had been tested before."

And that, Malka, was what Katriel was telling me that night, before the final assault on the Old City. But do you know who the beggar was? Sometimes I tell myself he was Katriel, he was I.

XV

U P   B E F O R E   dawn, we gulped a
few swallows of boiling coffee and climbed into half-tracks.
To the front a mile away. Preoccupied, the men avoided
conversation. Some were thinking of companions already
lost along the way, or of those about to be lost. Others, their
helmets on their knees, were scribbling farewell messages to
wives or parents.

The minutes grew longer, time was suspended. In con-
fronting the enemy or death, waiting is far worse than racing
under fire. What goes through one's mind when, poised on
the edge of destiny, one strains to precipitate events? Not
the future. One retraces one's steps into time, allowing one's
fantasy free reign. One corrects the past. Called to the blackboard, I reply yes rather than no, and am congratulated by
the teacher. Finding myself at a crossroads one sordid morning, I veer to the right rather than the left, and my existence
shifts patterns. A few precise if childish memories demand
reviewing: you offended a certain neighbor, you did not
pay the laundry, you did not return a certain book to the
library.

And Katriel? He had closed the door to the outside world.
Sullen, irritable again, what was he thinking about? The fact
that he would have to kill again, this time for Jerusalem?

The night weighed like a burning on my eyelids. Suddenly

a tremor ran through me. High above, a cloud changed course and broke in two. As I lowered my head, I saw Katriel staring at me. I was going to ask him why, but he didn't give me a chance.

"Listen," he said, trembling. "I've a favor to ask of you."

"Yes?"

"Don't stay next to me."

"But, Katriel! Our pact!"

"Please, I beg you!"

There was such anguish, such despair in his voice that I could not refuse. "I understand," I said, forcing a smile.

Don't hold it against him, Malka. You too must try to understand: it isn't easy to go mad while killing before witnesses.

"IS THERE still room for me?"

"We'll manage."

Standing in the command car, Gad was conferring with his staff. With a leap, I was beside him. As I looked over the surrounding countryside, I almost shouted with wonder.

The half-track was parked on a plateau from which at a single glance one could take in the ramparts and the citadel, with its turrets obscure and menacing. On the other side, looming in the purplish dusk, the Old City stood out in bold relief; one could clearly distinguish its domes, its minarets, its low, scorched houses.

"For you," said the radioman, handing Gad the earphones.

The message was addressed to the entire division:

"From the Division Commander to all officers and parachutists. We are beginning to ascend to the Old City. We shall liberate the Mount and the Temple Wall. The Jewish people are waiting for this victory and we shall rise to their expectation. The hours we are about to live will belong to Israel's history and legend. Good luck."

Gad was still holding on to the earphones long after the message had come to an end.

"You will remember this dawn," he said to me, unable to conceal his emotion.

"It's daylight already."

He looked at his watch as if to check me. "True, it's daylight."

Unexpectedly, church bells began to toll, as they had tolled once, long ago, in the land of my childhood. A shudder went through us: how could we trust our ears, our eyes? Peaceful, powerful, melodious sounds hovering over roads and fields strewn with corpses. And what if this were only a dream after all? What if I had never left my house, my garden, my friends?

"Gad," I said. "Where are we?"

"You'll learn soon."

His hand shading his eyes, he scanned the sky and the horizon. As if obeying his command, three or four or five jet squadrons appeared. At the same moment guns and mortars went into action. Heaven and earth seemed locked in a fierce competition, as if striving to prove which could generate the most fire or unleash the most deadly destruction.

"That's for us," said the radioman.

In a cutting voice, Gad gave his orders to the company commanders taking part in the assault. Through his field glasses he coolly watched the encircling attack for which he alone was responsible. The reports he received and relayed to GHQ were improving constantly. The initial thrust was followed up successfully. All units were progressing toward their given targets. The breakthrough would occur sooner than expected. Suddenly I saw Gad straighten up, adjust his helmet with a determined sweep.

"I've had enough of seeing all this from afar," he informed GHQ. "We're going too."

The driver, who had already started the engine, stepped on the accelerator. The half-track, after a nervous jump, shot forward, racing down the road.

"We're going," Gad repeated as if to himself.

No need to ask for details. Everything was becoming very clear, very simple. Taut with anticipation, carried away, almost blinded by emotion, we looked straight ahead, not daring to breathe normally. Excitement had taken possession of all our senses. Never mind obstacles or snipers. Caught up in the event, at the mercy of the elements, we were flying toward fire and battle, and all our thoughts were concentrated on speed, this new god whom we must appease. A cry, always the same, burnt our lips and echoed in the distance: "We're going, we're going!"

We were shouting louder and louder so as to be heard by foe and friend alike, over the whistling of bullets, the howling of mortars, the groaning of the wounded, the final gasps of the dying. We were in the midst of a demented hell, with heaven and earth gone insane. We didn't know then that we were shouting to be heard by the whole world, by centuries past and future; we were shouting to· tumble down the walls, to liberate the city and the Wall, symbol of its eternity; we were shouting to convince ourselves that the voices were our voices, the dreams our dreams, and that we were catching up with them.

And in the nightmarish dawn of a day just born, I saw soldiers arriving from everywhere, gripped by the same urge to shout and cry; they were coming by car and on foot, running or dragging themselves, seemingly unaware of their injuries, buttoned up tight in their scorched battle gear, their blackened helmets covering their eyes, and all converging in the same direction, toward the same rallying point, the same gate: I thought I heard the roaring of lions.

I leaned over to Gad. "Have we all gone mad?" I screamed into his ear.

"I warned you, didn't I? The madmen have taken things into their hands."

And there we were in the Old City. Dark, narrow alleys, one running into the other. Buildings with leprous façades. Windows boarded up. Barricades ground to dust. A child crying somewhere. From a rooftop, a legionnaire, having thrown a cluster of grenades, came crashing down in front of us, his arms dangling. Farther on, someone fired a machine gun; the response was a shower of flames. A few steps away, a little girl, frozen with fear, stood in a half-open doorway.

The shooting was continuing without respite. There was fighting in every house, in every courtyard. The enemy had adopted new tactics. Rear-guard fighting instead of organized resistance. The place was teeming with isolated soldiers who, having survived the first onslaught, crawled out of hiding and attacked our flanks. They would be dealt with later. The mopping-up had to wait.

"Faster, faster," Gad was shouting, and so were we.

Unbelievable but true: Gad himself had been swept into the mass delirium. His cool composure was gone. There was a new ecstatic gleam in his eyes. Only then did I notice the layer of black soot on his face. Was it really Gad under that mask? I would have to check later, not now. Even Gad could wait.

Unexpectedly we came upon an open space which seemed to climb to the sky: the Har Habayit, the Temple Mount.

Strange but true: Division Commander Colonel Motta Gur was there before us. He had been the first to arrive, before his scouts. Trembling with pride—a new kind of pride, resembling anger—he was shouting, over and over, into his radio: "The Har Habayit is in our hands! Do you hear? The Temple Mount is in our hands!" Yes, they heard him at the other end of the line, they heard him at the other end of the world.

A transfigured Gad ordered the driver to back up and enter a side street winding around the sacred hill. Here too, no need to explain. Next objective, next stop: the Wall. We would be among the first there, but we would not be alone. Others were running on the same road, obeying the same impulse. A barricade, seemingly improvised—planks and tables—was quickly overturned. Another barricade. The next street proved too narrow for our vehicle. Too bad. Leaving the driver and a corporal behind, the rest of us, Gad in the lead, entered it on foot, racing. We were joined on the way by large numbers of soldiers and officers, coming out of nowhere and everywhere. Occasionally one could see an old Arab peeking from behind a poorly camouflaged window, watching the massive rush in amazement. Here and there we were pelted with bullets and shell fragments. Some of us were hit while running, they were picked up and carried along; we would dress their wounds later. No one killed? Not that I know of. For the duration of the race, death had relinquished its hold on us. Later it would catch up. Not now. Death too had to wait.

"Look!" someone shouted. "Look! The Wall!"

Another cry, then a third: "The Wall! Right here!"

And all of us: "Look! Loo-oo-k!"

Then everything stopped. Breath, life, the sun. War itself

stood still. Afraid that I had been deceived, I didn't dare come closer. I had to force myself to look.

I had never seen the Wall before, yet I recognized it. I looked at it as one looks at someone from whom one has been forcibly separated a long time, perhaps forever.

The sensation of living inside a dream was still with me. Indeed it was growing stronger. One part of me was stunned and suspicious. I knew this was the Wall, but I couldn't believe that it was really I standing there and contemplating it. The victor in me was as alien to me as he was unreal.

"To follow tradition, we ought to be tearing our clothes," said someone behind me.

Katriel had aged during the night. He fell into my arms.

"Our sages command it," he went on, stressing each word. "Whoever sees the Wall must go into mourning in memory of the destroyed Temple. I'm sure my father would do it if he were here, if he could see."

He suppressed a sob. "Only I won't. Not today. Today is not meant for mourning. When you meet my father, you must tell him."

And after a silence: "You will also tell him that in order to get here this morning, we all had to tear our clothing."

He didn't give me time to ask him whether he had any message for you, Malka, or whether our pact was still in effect. He already had something else on his mind.

"Paper," he said. "You need paper."

"What?!"

"You must write something."

"Are you crazy? Write what?"

"A wish. Custom demands it. You write a wish and slip it between the cracks of the Wall."

He handed me a scrap of paper and a pencil. I was not

prepared and so I searched for words, for names. What wish should I formulate, and for whom? The disciples for whom the Baal Shem Tov had interceded had simply asked for good health, both of body and soul. Well, I could follow their example. I could try. I wrote my name: David ben Sarah, David, son of Sarah. And my hand refused to continue. Once upon a time it had been my mother—Sarah, daughter of Doved—who had written the requests and solicited for me, for us, the intercession of the holy and the just, and had wished me to resemble them.

"Haven't you finished? Hurry!"

Katriel's request was ready. No, Malka, I don't know its contents. I don't know what he asked for you. I saw him approach the Wall and carefully insert his crumpled piece of paper between the stones. As for me, I still didn't know what to write. What could I ask for myself? And from whom? I thought of scribbling: "Lord, have pity on Your creation as well as on Yourself." But the name of my mother presented an unsurmountable obstacle.

In the general tumult Gad disappeared and so did Katriel. Gad fell shortly thereafter, but that I only learned later. Alone, separated from my friends, I didn't know what advice to ask, nor from whom.

And then I heard a voice inside me saying:

"I am the eye that looks at the eye that is looking. I shall look so hard that I shall be blinded. Then I shall sing. I shall sing with such force that I shall go mad. Then I shall dream.

"I shall dream that I am David, son of Sarah. I tell my mother what I have done with her tears and her prayers. I tell her what I have done with my years and my silences and my life. Why so late? I had no strength. I could not accept your absence. If I have never written you, it is because I have never left you. You were the one who went away, and ever since, I see you going away. I see nothing else. For years now, you have been leaving me, vanishing into the distance, swallowed by the black and silent tide, but the sky that drowned the fire cannot drown you. You are the fire, you are the sky. And this hand which is writing, it is stretched toward you. And this vision which haunts me, it is my offering to you. And the silence, it is on your lips I find it and give it back. Wandering beggar or prisoner, it is always your voice I seek to set free inside me. And each time I address myself to strangers, I am speaking to you."

So I contemplate the Wall which bears my mother's face. Yes, she had two faces, my mother. One showed the daily sorrows from Sunday to Friday, the other reflected the serenity of Shabbat. And now, this is the only one she has left.

A human throng presses toward the Wall, nestles against it. I stand aside and look.

In a flash I see from one end of the world to the other, and further, into my deepest self. I see all those who had stood here before me, bent with humility or touched with ecstasy. Here, before this very Wall. Kings and prophets, warriors and priests, poets and philosophers, rich and poor, all those who throughout the ages had pleaded everywhere for a little compassion, a little kindness: it was here they came to speak of it.

Here, in this place, a sage of Israel once remarked, the stones are souls; it is they who each day rebuild an invisible temple. Still, it is not here that I will find my mother's soul. The soul of my mother found shelter in fire and not in stone. And to think that her own dream had been to come here and pray and meditate and cry. Well then, I shall dream in her place.

But that army chaplain who is approaching, Torah in hand, like a bridegroom on his wedding day, where had I seen him before? Tears are streaming down his face as he recites a prayer and blows the shofar. And that horn itself, did it not come from a ram sacrificed on this very spot four thousand years ago by a father crushed by faith and love? And is not that father also present here? And the chaplain? Could he be the angel who took pity on Abraham and saved him by saving his son? If so, then for once God is on the side of man, on the side of madmen.

And that old Hasid who comes running, where have I seen him before? Dressed in a black kaftan and black felt hat, his prayer shawl under his arm, he hurls himself against the Wall as if to smash his head. Hypnotized by the stones, he feels them, caresses them and sobs inwardly, without shedding a tear. For a moment I observe him as if he were a stone among the stones. Then I see soldiers lifting him up, tossing him into the air, yelling: "You must not weep, not any more; the time for lamentations is over; we must rejoice, old man, we must cry our joy to the Wall, it needs that joy and so do we." One circle is formed, then another. Everyone is dancing, and on a carpet of shoulders, the old man is dancing too. He is not afraid of falling, or of flying away, he is not afraid of anything and neither are we. Someone breaks into song, and that song fills the square, the city and the whole country. "Louder, louder," the old man shouts, bouncing back each time with new vigor, greater frenzy; he is in ecstasy and so are we. Someone near me succumbs to tears. Someone is weeping, and it's not I. Someone is weeping and it is I. And in my dream, through my tears, I see the old man lift his arms, trying to tear away a scrap of sky: an offering to those who sing, to those who make him tall and proud and invincible. Who is he? King

David perhaps? Abraham? Or Katriel? Or perhaps the Messiah?

I know I ought to be afraid: the miracle is too violent, the joy too intense. It cannot last forever. But I also know that I am dreaming. I am at the top of a mountain, I trip over a pebble, I fall, I see the abyss growing darker as it approaches, darker than the dark eye of the tempest. I am afraid, but fear itself is part of the dream.

Let it continue then.

It is still early. The sun hangs seemingly motionless over the stones made sacred by men. A solemn melody of long ago soars over the city and floats down the Valley of Jehoshaphat; and yet my soul—yes, don't laugh—my soul does not even feel the need or the desire to follow, not even to escape that which endangers it.

From afar I see the dancers set the old man down. They are exhausted, he is not. And now I can distinguish his features more clearly. A familiar face. He is the beggar, the preacher of my childhood. He recognizes me and beckons. I tear myself from the ground and take one step toward him, then another. I sigh with relief: it is not he, it is a younger man. Could it be Katriel? A crowd separates us, I do my best to rejoin him, but he disappears from sight. I question people: "Where did he go, that tall, slender man with burning eyes, the one about my age?" They don't know. In panic I run from one person to another. Some turn their backs, others stare at me, their eyes blank.

Meanwhile, the crowd keeps getting larger. Military personnel and officials, celebrities and journalists, all are streaming by in one continuous procession, along with rabbis and students, gathered from all over the city, from every corner of the land. Men, women and adolescents of every age, every origin and speaking every language, and I see them ascend-

ing toward the Wall, toward all that remains of their collective longing. Just like long ago, at Sinai, when they were
given the Torah. Just like a generation ago, in the kingdom
of night, when it was taken back. Once again the exiles are
being gathered in, the knot is being knotted—the end is
rejoining the beginning and justifying it. Over there, in
the camp, a wise and pious inmate had cried out in a fit of
madness: "All of us heard God in the desert; here we shall
be allowed to see Him." — "Yes," the others had answered,
"we shall see Him and perish." The image of God cannot
be transmitted; it can be carried away only in death.

Here, it is man's image that is being transmitted. And in
order to receive it, an entire people had begun to march for
the third time in its history.

It is always the same people, its march is always the same.
The setting too remains unchanged. The characters succeed
each other with hallucinating speed, like a series of super-
imposed pictures, each layer more ancient than the one
above. Scholars and aesthetes, princes and rebels intermin-
gling with rabbis dressed in black, soldiers in full battle gear,
enraptured Talmudic students and young girls in bloom:
their eyes, their arms laden with gifts and dreams. Begun
eternities ago, their march is that of men determined to make
their past and destiny their own.

That stooped, obstinate father with the scorched beard:
on what stake and in the name of what law did he endure
martyrdom? That bent-over adolescent: what joy was torn
from him? That little girl biting her nails: in which ghetto
and in which times did she acquire such maturity, so much
experience? She is approaching with small, measured steps,
and I wonder why she isn't running; she ought to be running
and growing up, she ought to be running away—to life.
She isn't running, because a woman is holding her arm; a

woman who walks slowly, with infinite dignity. Suddenly I see her profile, only her profile, and my heart jumps. A moment later I see them more distinctly. There can be no doubt. Her mouth open, the little girl is gasping for air, she is choking, she is thirsty, but she says nothing so as not to worry her mother, who is also mine.

Thus, by inviting hallucination and then rejecting it, I plunge into it and find friends, parents and neighbors, all the dead of the town, all the dead towns of the cemetery that was Europe. Here they are, at the timeless twilight hour, pilgrims all, invading the Temple of which they are both fiery foundation and guardians. Free enough, proud enough to have accepted leaving this world, they have now come back from far, very far, beyond the roofs and stars, from another time and other homes, wanting to live the beginning and the end of their tale. Nothing could stop them, not even the divine will restraining the Messiah. For they have no tombs to hold them back, no cemeteries to bind them to the earth; they have come down from the sky, their cemetery is the sky, and their eyes are eternity and its night.

I look at them and I am afraid to look, afraid to discover myself among them. I'll pretend not to have seen. I look and can't stop looking.

A father lifts his son to his shoulders and tells him to open his eyes wide. A young couple in love, holding hands, quicken their step. Two widows slow theirs down.

I shake myself and let reality speak: "You're mistaking the date if not the place! You haven't seen all this today! Agreed. But does it matter! I saw it another day, a week later, a month later. Time doesn't matter, only the tale does. Besides, I am not the only one to have seen and to see still. A man, his arms folded, is also watching the crowd. Now I know who he is. I am positive. He is the wandering preacher bringing silence where it is needed, when it is needed. Somber and severe, taller and straighter than in life, he is conversing with a disciple who, curiously, resembles him: "Do you know why Jerusalem was saved?" — "No. Why?" — "Because this time the towns and the villages, large and small alike, by the hundreds and thousands, rose up in its defense."

As always, he tells the truth. Not far from here, in a cave, the Martef Hashoa, the visitor can find their names, only their names, endless names, some heavy with glory, others difficult to retain and pronounce, all etched deeply into the black stone: that is all that remains.

These towns and villages, emptied of their Jews, these names severed from their life source, had joined forces and built a safety curtain—an Amud Esh, a pillar of fire—around the city which had given them a home. Sighet and Lodz, Vilna and Warsaw, Riga and Bialystok, Drancy and Bratzlav: Jerusalem had once again become the memory of an entire people.

"And the dead," the preacher was saying in a vibrant voice. "The messenger who is alive today, the victor of today, would be wrong to forget the dead. Israel defeated its enemies—do you know why? I'll tell you. Israel won because its army, its people, could deploy six million more names in battle."

And to the young woman who is looking at me instead of contemplating the shadows around the Wall, I say: "Now, Malka, do you know what the Jews did to win this war?"

She wrinkles her brow: "Yes, now I know."

Then I turn toward her and look into her eyes: "Know also that I never saw Katriel again."

She holds my gaze and says: "I know, yes, I know that too."

XVI

A MAN, over there.

Do you see him? Sitting on a tree stump, he watches from the side as the shadows gather and separate in silence beneath the ramparts before evacuating the square at the break of dawn. Soon they will depart, in clusters, to seek refuge in the childhood of old men, in the mute obsessions of orphans.

Morning will soon be here. The sun will sprinkle its purple dust over the constantly changing countryside and its blood over the domes, the towers, the battlements, while setting ablaze the mountains suspended between heaven and earth.

This is the hour when emptiness surrounds me. The visitors have gone home, the guard has been changed. My companions depart alone or in groups of twos and threes. Clumsy beggars, light-footed madmen, some laugh, others scowl. Before going their separate ways, they hold counsel and divide the world among themselves, deciding who will take possession of what on that particular day.

One will go to the synagogue, another to the market, the cemetery, the library, the hospital and—why not?—the theater. Will the prince return to his kingdom beyond the Sambatyon? Will Shlomo, the blind Hasid, meet someone worth listening to? And by consoling his hungry suppliers, will Anshel feel less guilty? Perhaps I shall know the answers one day, perhaps tomorrow, if there is a tomorrow.

"I'd like to go home," Malka says. "Come with me. You need rest and so do I."

Her hair is disheveled, her features are blurred and her lips faded; she pities herself, and like all scorned women she is to be pitied.

"I can't go on," she whispers. "I'm exhausted. Please: the trial has lasted long enough. Come, let's go home."

Poor Malka. Does she know how difficult it is to retrace one's steps? She does. And it doesn't discourage her. What could I answer? I choose not to listen.

Besides, here come the first worshippers, the first pilgrims. The first morning service. Some of the regulars, always the same, are present. Pinhas the Recluse, who twenty years ago locked himself in his home and took a vow not to leave it until the Old City was freed. Not long ago an officer knocked on his door: "Reb Pinhas, you may come out." A few steps farther, Baruch the Mute, his head thrown back, his lips moving, seems to be asking heaven for permission to break his silence at last. He too was fetched in a military jeep. He refused to climb in. At first he stared at the officer without understanding; then, without blinking or changing expression, he started running like one possessed, paying no attention to the gunfire all around, and, strangely, he reached the Wall before the jeep. A third worshipper, no less familiar: Guiladi. Sad and taciturn, he had been the last defender to leave this neighborhood after its fall. Now he prowls around it for hours on end. And Katriel, where is he? Perhaps the dead have taken him along.

Is it fatigue or lack of sleep? I feel the wound reopening. From the depth of the abyss, the years soar up, unchecked, snatching my heart and pounding it violently against my chest. Anguish grips me, as though I were about to meet something as absolute, as decisive, as pure as the death of a child at dawn. I look at my wife, I touch her and I love loving her, yet something in me shrivels and rebels. And I am seized by an irresistible urge to walk. To walk without respite, without reason, without catching my breath, day after day, night after night, my throat parched, my eyes open wide; to walk so as to punish my body for keeping time imprisoned, and punish my spirit for having resisted; to walk so as to reach, beyond exhaustion, that level of awareness on which mirrors shatter into a thousand pieces and each piece into a thousand reflections, to walk so as to die while walking, and too bad if in the end one must live again and remember. But Katriel stops me, it is he who judges me.

Look at me, Malka. Look closely and tell me whom you see; I don't know any more. Tell me if you are waiting for Katriel as I am waiting for him. Katriel: was that even his name? Yes or no, it hardly matters: that was the name he flaunted to exorcise a threat, to ingratiate himself with that which is present but unseen. Sometimes, contented, he would enunciate it slowly, solemnly: probing it, savoring it. Other times he would angrily, bitterly blurt it out as though to dispose of it. At night, under the open sky, he made it a complaint, a farewell song, using it to pry a crack in his own armor, or to follow to the end a vision, an impulse. In daylight he would regard his name as a toy, a disguise. Rare and unpredictable, his absences were brief. A few seconds, no more. Just long enough to enter another man's consciousness, to pull himself together: "Katriel, you must not." Then there would be torture in his eyes. And it had no name.

But I notice that I am speaking of him in the past tense. I should not. Katriel has gone away, he may still come back.

One day he will have had enough and he will reappear, under another identity, more mysterious and more invincible too, and he will tell Katriel the adventures of Katriel. "Have I come too late?" he will ask. Crying and laughing, Malka, you will nod gracefully: "Yes, you have come too late, much too late."

And the beggar, having waited for him until the end, will add: "Yes, too late to laugh, too late for tears." It is only to tell him this that he has stayed here for more than a week, more than a month. His body, bent and chill, he feels old, older than the old men, his Masters of long ago whose blessing still torments him: "One day, son, the madmen in you will be appeased. And on that day . . ." They died, willing him their unfinished promise. He never stopped asking them for a continuation, for an end: I have journeyed across the earth and come to rest in this place where time at last welcomes me instead of expelling me; my thirst quenched with legends gathered from your lips, I dwell in them and add some of my own; I cross destinies and borders, collecting them on the way. But the key to peace, why did you entrust it to Katriel?

And you, Malka, why don't you trust me? Why do you pull away? Don't try to bind me with fear. Or pity. Your life is not in danger, it is a beggar who tells you so. Unlike Adam, whom God permitted to plunge into the future and know the very last of his descendants, I shall show you the past and its origins. Don't be afraid to listen, Malka. Someone is singing: it is David weeping over Absalom's death. Someone is weeping: it is Jeremiah predicting the destruction of the indestructible city. Someone is shouting: it is Rabbi Akiba exorcising misfortune by laughing. Someone becomes a murmur: it is Yehuda Halevi, lover and poet of Zion, whose soul penetrates the stone and thereby retains its trembling; it is a child asking questions of his grandfather: "It is written that the Shekhinah, the divine presence, never leaves Jerusalem; but it is also written that it follows the Jews, all the Jews, into exile: isn't there a contradiction in that?" And the grandfather answers: "That proves the Shekhinah is present even within contradictions."

"What do you want, what do you expect of me?"

You don't know, Malka; neither do I. The beggar does not ask you for alms, he has no use for charity. He simply asks you to look at him, to look at him closely; he needs this to find himself, to define himself. Look at him and tell me if his face belongs to him and to him alone. He doesn't remember it. Perhaps it was stolen from him like his other selfs. If only he could imagine Katriel killed or mute, everything would become simple: he would know what to do. But his imagination rebels: I can't see Katriel other than alive. His disappearance proves nothing, except that certain stories don't have an ending. Or a beginning.

Oh yes, with Katriel dead, I would know how to act: I would tear him away from death. But with Katriel alive, have I the right to act as though he were not, and speak and live in his stead? How can I convince myself that it is his wish, not mine, that drives me to speak of his memories and his obsessions, which I find difficult to distinguish from my own? And then, this thought which keeps coming back, chilling my blood: What if I am dead and he is the survivor?

"Come with me," Malka begs. "Leave the past alone. The dead have no right in Jerusalem. They shouldn't even stay overnight."

"And Katriel?" I ask, hurt.

"Let Katriel be."

"And what if he comes back?"

Malka keeps silent, discouraged: everything has been said.

Dawn melts into the mist. Heaven and earth embrace before separating. Somewhere, someone sick stirs and moans: the angel has not yet stolen his eyes. A dog barks and the sound reverberates mysteriously in the distance. To console herself, a widow invents a reason to hope. On the ramparts, the guards chat in subdued tones. The city shakes itself awake, opens its shutters and goes about its business. Watchman, what of life? What of victory? Gone the watchman. But I will not answer in his place.

Somewhere a storyteller is bent over a photograph taken by a German, an officer fond of collecting souvenirs. It shows a father and his son, in the middle of a human herd, moving toward the ditch where, a moment later, they will be shot. The father, his left hand on the boy's shoulder, speaks to him gently while his right hand points to the sky. He is explaining the battle between love and hatred: "You see, my child, we are right now losing that battle." And since the boy does not answer, his father continues: "Know, my son, if gratuitous suffering exists, it is ordained by divine will. Whoever kills, becomes God. Whoever kills, kills God. Each murder is a suicide, with the Eternal eternally the victim."

And the survivor in all this? He will end up writing his request, which he will slip between the cracks of the Wall. Addressed to the dead, it will ask them to take pity on a world which has betrayed and rejected them. Being powerful and vindictive, they can do whatever they please. Punish. Or even forgive.

But don't worry. A page has been turned. The beasts in the heart of man have stopped howling, they have stopped bleeding. The curse has been revoked in this place and its reign terminated. To kill or to be killed no longer assures glory or saintliness. The warriors have returned to their homes, the dead to their tombs. The orphans are learning to smile again, the victors to weep. Yes, the war is over, and the beggar knows it. He is alone, but that he doesn't know.

The square is getting crowded. The usual: strollers, visitors, guides. This way, gentlemen. Hurry, ladies, please. For the thousandth time, in every imaginable language, I hear the same explanations recited in the same artificially excited tones: "This is the Mosque of Omar: it is from here that Mohammed and his horse flew to heaven. And here is the tomb of Christ. Weep, admire, set your cameras, smile: thank you. Come on, look as if you're thrilled, moved, impressed: thank you, thank you."

Her clothes rumpled, her mouth pasty, Malka ignores the mob around her. She could pretend to look for Katriel; she doesn't. She could stroke my aching temples and tell me that all wounds heal; she doesn't. And I am grateful. She knows, as I do, that it would be a waste.

She smiles shyly: "Do you want me to go away?"

"Yes."

"Do you want me to come back?"

"Yes."

She says "Good" and stands up. She rearranges her skirt, puts on her kerchief and leaves without looking at me. I watch her make her way through the crowd, determined, as if knowing where to go and whom to meet. And I see myself again on the day of our marriage. Only ten people present, the *minyan* required for the ceremony. Strangers. On the verge of tears, I had told her: "Sorry, Malka. Our guests were not able to come."

"When your tale will be told you . . ." Yes, the prediction is proved correct. This war too will have left its mark on the lives of more than one person. Someone died inside me, I still don't know who. But I do know this: Whether Katriel is alive or not is not important. I shall unlearn being jealous of his past, of his innocence. What is important is to continue. It will take time and patience: the beggar knows how to wait.

Yet one of these days he will have to decide, put an end to his waiting and go away too. But where? Home, of course, but he still doesn't know where that is. A woman is getting ready to welcome him, but he still doesn't know who she is. Tomorrow, or the week after, he will finally have to retrace his steps and erase their imprint, but he has forgotten the road back: no one walks it with impunity.

A victor, he? Victory does not prevent suffering from having existed, nor death from having taken its toll. How can one work for the living without by that very act betraying those who are absent? The question remains open, and no new fact can change it. Of course, the mystery of good is no less disturbing than the mystery of evil. But one does not cancel out the other. Man alone is capable of uniting them by remembering.

While accepting ambiguity and the quest arising from it, the beggar at times would like to lose his memory; he can not. On the contrary: it keeps growing and swelling, storing away events and faces until the past of others becomes one with his own. By continued survival, he no longer differentiates between his allies, his ghosts and his guides, and whether he owes them allegiance. For him everything is question, including the miracle that keeps him on the surface.

That is why I am still here on this haunted square, in this city where nothing is lost and nothing dispersed. An indispensable, necessary transition. To catch my breath. To become accustomed to a situation whose newness still makes me dizzy. During this time I do not count the hours or the men. I watch them go by. The beggar in me could detain them, he lets them pass. He could follow them, he lets them pass. Katriel did perhaps exist, and the beggar did not follow him.

For tales, like people, all have the same beginning.

Jerusalem 1967 —
Christiansted 1968

BOOKS BY ELIE WIESEL

Available from Schocken

A BEGGAR IN JERUSALEM

In the days following the Six-Day War, a Holocaust survivor visits the reunited city of Jerusalem. At the Western Wall he encounters the beggars and madmen who congregate there every evening, and who force him to confront the ghosts of his past and his ties to the present.

THE GATES OF THE FOREST

A young Jew hiding from the Nazis in the forests and small towns of Eastern Europe allows another refugee to sacrifice himself in his stead. As he struggles with his guilt, one question recurs: How to live in a world that God has abandoned?

LEGENDS OF OUR TIME

From a rabbi at Auschwitz who fasts on Yom Kippur, to a young Spanish Catholic whose discovery of an ancient Marrano document starts him on a quest to regain his lost heritage, Wiesel's encounters with fifteen extraordinary men and women resonate with the poetry and passion of Jewish spiritual resistance.

THE TOWN BEYOND THE WALL

Based on Wiesel's own life, this is the story of a young Holocaust survivor who returns to his hometown after the liberation, seeking to understand the mystery of what he calls "the face in the window"—the symbol of all those who just stood by and watched as innocent men, women, and children were led to the slaughter.

THE TRIAL OF GOD

When three itinerant actors arrive in a small Eastern European village to perform a Purim play for the Jewish community, they are horrified to discover that all but two of the Jewish residents have been murdered in a recent pogrom. The actors decide to stage a mock trial of God, indicting Him for allowing such things to happen to His children.

Available from Vintage

A JEW TODAY

In this powerful collection of essays, letters, and diary entries, Wiesel probes such central moral and political issues as Zionism and the Middle East conflict, anti-Semitism in the former U.S.S.R., the obligations of American Jews toward Israel, and the media's treatment of the Holocaust.

AVAILABLE AT YOUR LOCAL BOOKSTORE *or*

To order by mail, please fill out or copy the form below and send to:
Random House Order Department,
400 Hahn Road, Westminster, Maryland 21157.
To order by phone, call 1-800-733-3000 (credit cards only).

- If you wish to pay by check or money order, please make it payable to Random House, Inc.
- If you prefer to charge your order to a major credit card, please fill in the information below.

Charge my account with

❏ American Express   ❏ Visa   ❏ MasterCard

Account No. _____ Expiration Date _____

(Signature) _____

Name _____

Address _____

City/State/Zip _____

TITLE	ISBN	QUANTITY	PRICE	TOTAL
A Beggar in Jerusalem	0-8052-0897-6	_____ x	$14.00	= _____
The Gates of the Forest	0-8052-0896-8	_____ x	$13.00	= _____
A Jew Today	0-394-74057-2	_____ x	$ 9.00	= _____
Legends of Our Time	0-8052-0714-7	_____ x	$14.00	= _____
The Town Beyond the Wall	0-8052-0697-3	_____ x	$13.00	= _____
The Trial of God	0-8052-0809-7	_____ x	$12.00	= _____
		Shipping/Handling*	=	_____
		Subtotal	=	_____
		Sales Tax (where applicable)	=	_____
		Total Enclosed	= $	_____

*In addition to the price of the books, enclose shipping and handling: $2.00 for the first book and $0.50 for each additional book ordered.

Prices subject to change without notice. Please allow 4-6 weeks for delivery.